D1446655

VIOLET'S WISH

VIOLET'S WISH

•

Carolyn Brown

AVALON BOOKS
NEW YORK

PRINTED IN THE UNITED STATES OF AMERICA
ON ACID-FREE PAPER
BY HADDON CRAFTSMEN, BLOOMSBURG, PENNSYLVANIA

This book is dedicated to
my sons-in-law
Bobby Rucker
and Mike Harmon
. . . with much love!

Chapter One

The sun set over the rolling hills in a bright orange ball, sinking lower and lower. As low as Violet's heart. Was life never going to be anything but dull, dull, dull? She watched the day ebb away into twilight and gave herself a strong lecture. She had friends, a home, a life, even if it was the same thing day after day. And she was independent. In 1891, independence was certainly something a lot of women would never have.

As if the Oklahoma wildflowers couldn't contain their beauty out in the open fields, the blossoms had come right into the town of Dodsworth. Everywhere a wildflower could grow, it sprouted in the red earth. Dodsworth looked like a patchwork quilt. Indian paintbrush, buttercups, Indian blanket, black-eyed Susans, and a multitude of other blossoms in bright colors claimed even the smallest of corners. Violet looked back over her life. It, too, had been like a quilt. A patch of happiness here. A massive heartache sewn smack dab in the middle. Another bit of sorrow tucked in there. A lot of blah squares.

1

"What're you thinkin' about so hard that it makes your eyebrows almost grow together?" Jim Parsons asked.

Jim had thinning, light brown hair he kept parted perfectly. His nondescript brown eyes lacked sparkle. But he was as solid as a brick wall, and everyone said that's what a woman should look for in a husband. Everyone but Violet. She'd had that in Zeb. She wanted that breathless feeling she'd known once when she was a young woman in Texas. That crazy emotional ride like her heart was on a bucking bronc.

"Just life in general," Violet said. She couldn't hurt Jim's feelings by telling him he was as lackluster as everything else in her life. After Zeb's death last year she'd made herself a solemn vow she'd never get involved with another man who was so passive. They'd been married eight years and never once had a fight. Never had a single valley experience in their marriage, or a top of the mountain experience either, for that matter. Their whole marriage had run in the same narrow rut until she'd just figured that was what married life was supposed to be like. Then Emma came to Dodsworth, and Violet envied her and Jed their rocky relationship. They fought. They cried. They laughed. They kissed and made up. Even after a year of marriage and a baby on the way, Emma said they still couldn't go a week without an argument. But with a wink, she'd confided in Violet she sometimes started a fight just so they could go to the bedroom and make up.

Violet watched the sun fade into twilight. That's what she wanted. A relationship like her best friend, Emma, had with her husband, Jed. Their eyes glittered when they spoke about each other, and when Emma was away those months the previous summer, Jed had walked around like half his soul was gone. If she ever married again, Violet didn't want a man she could live with. She wanted one she couldn't live without, no matter how much they disagreed.

"So what about life?" Jim said after they'd ridden another block down the main street of Dodsworth, from the church to her house on the south side of town.

"It's kind of like living in a rut most of the time, isn't it?" she said absentmindedly.

"That's what life is, Violet. It's workin' and makin' a livin' and I guess it would seem like a rut to some folks. Now, me, I figure it this way. A body works and lives right and when the end comes they go on to Heaven and rest in peace forever more," Jim said in a voice without any inflection. No eagerness. No passion. Just a monotone. Even worse than Zeb's voice had been.

"Seems like there ought to be more to it," Violet said as he drew the reins in on the horse and stopped the buggy in front of her house. It was a white frame house with a wide front porch complete with a swing—an extravagance two years since the land run. Folks still lived in dugouts as they tried to force crops out of the red earth and make improvements on their property. Zeb had been a good husband in that respect. He paid to have a house built for her, painted it white himself, and built the porch swing.

Jim just shook his head in bewilderment. Women were always looking for something exciting and happy. Look at Emma, that southern lady Jed married. First she come to Dodsworth to be his wife, then up and went back to Atlanta. Then all of a sudden here she was in church with him again. Jim guessed Jed got her lined out proper now, because she was about to have a baby and hadn't run back home to Georgia again. He hopped down and slowly walked around the back of the buggy.

Violet waited impatiently, wanting to get out of the buggy on her own without his help. Nothing hurried Jim Parsons. That's what Maggie said last Sunday after church. She'd giggled and said that a hive of bumble bees couldn't hurry him up. He had two speeds: slow and stop. Finally after what seemed like hours he reached up to put his hands properly around her waist and lift her down from the seat.

A fleeting vision of him taking her in his arms and kissing her passionately flitted across her mind. Wouldn't it be a miracle if he did, and there was a fire there. Even if they had a spark in only one area of their lives, maybe she could bear the rut he lived in. But when she was safely on the ground, he respectfully dropped his hands away from her and shoved them into the pockets of his Sunday trousers.

"Well, here we are at your house. I'm glad you let me drive you home, Violet. You know Zeb's been gone a year now, and I'd like to come callin' proper like. Maybe take you out for a drive on a Saturday evenin'. Maybe even you could make us up a picnic and we could drive up to the creek bank and eat it," he said, still without an ounce of excitement in his voice.

"Well." Violet searched for the right words to keep from hurting his feelings. Jim Parsons was even more stable than Preacher Elgin. He wouldn't ever break her heart like someone else had done back in Blue Ridge, Texas, all those years ago. But that incident was buried deep in her past and she rarely thought about those days. Jim would never make her heart thump so hard it felt like it would beat right out of her chest, either. It seemed to her it was the same story she'd already lived with Zeb all over again, just a different man. "To tell the truth, Jim, I just don't think I'm quite ready for courting just yet. I need a little more time. Folks say a year is proper and I expect I'm not getting any younger, but I'm just not ready."

"I'll abide by that. Wouldn't never want you to feel like I rushed you. I'll be seeing you at church then next Sunday, Violet," he said, tipping his hat.

"Sure thing," she mumbled to his back.

She slung her shawl over the back of a chair when she crossed the living room. She stopped long enough to look at her reflection in the full-length mirror on the back of her bedroom door. It was the only extravagant present Zeb ever gave her. He bought it in St. Louis when the train he worked on went through there and brought it home to her for Christmas the last year he was alive. The woman staring back at her had thick dark brown hair, light eyes the color of the sky just before snowfall . . . at least that's what Orrin said. There. She'd actually thought his name instead of side-skirting the issue of Orrin Wilde. That was history. Ancient history buried long ago.

She was too tall, but then so was Emma and Jed thought she was the most beautiful woman in the whole world. Nine months pregnant with their first child and he still looked at her like he could kiss her right there in church in front of Preacher Elgin, the whole congregation, and the Almighty, Himself. That's what Violet wanted. If she ever did let a man into her life, she fully well intended that he would look at her like Jed looked at Emma. Maybe she needed to run away and marry the first man she laid eyes on, she thought. That's what happened to Emma. She'd been raised up a southern lady in Atlanta, Georgia, and her father picked out a man she was supposed to marry. Emma wasn't having any part of it so she ran away and wound up married to Jed less than an hour after she got off the train in Guthrie, Oklahoma. It hadn't been an easy marriage, what with him having his dead sister's four kids to raise, but they were making a go of it. And Jed thought the sun just came up each morning to put highlights in Emma's blond hair.

Violet left the lady in the mirror and wandered aimlessly through the house. She picked up a gingerbread square in the kitchen but laid it down after the first bite. She sat down at the piano and tried to play a couple of hymns, but that didn't keep her attention very long either. She finally took her shoes off and tucked her feet up under her on the settee. She opened the book Emma lent her last week when she went out to the farm. She read two chapters, but when the clock struck nine she laid it aside and couldn't remember a thing she'd read. She picked up a collar and began to crochet picot-edged lace around it. Preacher Elgin might have an apoplexy fit if he knew she was working on Sunday, but she had a choice—either do something or go stark raving mad with boredom. It was too early to go to bed. Too late to go visiting Emma or even Maggie. She counted the stitches. One, two, three, four, five, six, seven. Double back and single crochet in the fifth stitch. Crochet five. Single crochet in the fifth chain of the previous loop.

She finished the collar and laid it aside. Wandered aimlessly to the piano and touched a key. The simple note carried through the house, acting like a magical key to open a box of memories Violet didn't want to think about. She'd bought the piano with the money she made from sewing the past two years. When it was delivered she sat down on the bench while Zeb waited in the doorway, his arms folded across his chest and a smile on his face. She'd played a hymn for him, but her soul begged her to play a fast dancing tune like she did on those hot summer nights in Blue Ridge, Texas.

On those sultry nights, Orrin would pick up the fiddle and the two of them made music for everyone in the area to kick up their heels to. His eyes would search for hers even in the middle of the song, telling her that everything about their lives was as matched as their music. As it turned out in the end, their music was all that matched.

She drew her hands away from the piano and went back to the settee, where she picked up a pocket and began to crochet lace around it. She couldn't bring back the excitement of youth, but she wasn't going to look forward to eternity with nothing but one cold monotonous day after the other.

"Lord, please," she prayed aloud. "Can't I have someone more fervent than Jim Parsons in my life? Someone with a twinkle in his eyes and a passion in his heart. Someone who'll put a glitter in my eyes and who'll wake my restless heart to . . ." The prayer floated unfinished toward the heavens. She couldn't say the words out loud but they were branded on her heart and God knew what she asked for. But then, she'd prayed fervently once before. She'd kneeled beside the altar and smelled the aroma of fresh roses as she pleaded. God said no. Who was she to think the answer would be any different eight years later, when essentially her crazy heart still ached for the same thing?

They were out there. He strained his ears until they ached and couldn't hear a thing. Not a single snort of a horse. Not a chuckle. But they were there. He could smell their greed and his own fear. Here he was on the last leg of his journey and they were there. He'd come the whole way from California without a single problem. At least not until he stopped in Enid.

Eight years he'd worked on the west coast. Working the claim his uncle had left him. The gold hadn't floated around in chunks, but it had panned out slowly until he had what he figured he needed to go back home and buy a farm. That's where his passion lay. In farming. Not in working from daylight to dark looking for gold. He'd build a cabin. He'd beg, borrow, or buy a couple of good coon dogs, maybe a good old blue tick hound to hunt turkey, and maybe just maybe there'd be a tall lass who'd be glad to walk through life on his arm. Wouldn't it be something if the love of his life hadn't married in all those years he'd been away. "No," he whispered. "Miracles like that don't happen to me."

Just to go home would have to be enough. Home. Blue Ridge, Texas. Right in the middle of the prettiest country God ever made, and where he'd been raised up until he was eighteen years old. The bluebonnets would be blooming this time of year. Matter of fact, the whole countryside would be colorful with buttercups, black-eyed Susans, Indian paintbrush, and Indian blanket. Eight long hard years he'd worked so he could go back home and they were out there trying to keep him from his dream. A dream he'd already paid a high price to obtain. He wasn't going to give it away now; not without a fight.

He doused the fire with the remnants of the pot of coffee he'd brewed earlier and kicked dirt over the embers until there was no more smoke. He'd ride east through the night, angling down south when the sun came up. They might give up and stop tailing him if he put that many hours between him and them. He shoved the blue granite coffee pot and mug into a saddle bag, checked the other saddle bags, and rode away from the comfortable camp. He'd be dead tired by morning, but at least he'd be far ahead of them.

There were four of them, all riding black horses and wearing dark colored trousers and shirts. Their hats were black and their skin a rich coffee color. Somehow they'd figured out he was carrying enough gold to start a bank of his own. When he rode out of Enid, he'd had an uneasy feeling and pulled up on a rise just out of town. They were following his trail and didn't even seem to care that he knew. He remembered the Mexican man who'd bought out his claim and wondered if he'd sent these men to rob him. More than likely they had followed him for days and days and just caught up with him in Enid, Oklahoma.

He circled Guthrie. Riding through town in the middle of the night could cause a fracas with the local law. He might have to explain why he was traveling with so much gold and could wind up in jail while the law checked every poster in the whole United States to see if he'd robbed a train or a stage coach. He'd left the town behind him and was riding east when he heard the first zing. The bullet hit a tree, slinging a chunk of bark into his chest.

He leaned over his horse's mane and spurred the animal on to a run, keeping at the edge of the scrub oak trees as much as possible so he wouldn't be a moonlit target for the four robbers. The second bullet nailed his hat to the ground beside him. That fired up a rage all the way down to his scuffed up boots. The hat was a good one, bought just a month before. Hardly even had a good sweat ring on the inside, yet. Lots of good miles left in that nice gray felt hat and now it was on the ground with a bullet through the crown. Looked like he was going to have to find a ravine and make a stand after all. Even with the best horse a man could ride, he was loosing ground fast.

The third was the charm. The bullet started plowing flesh in his right shoulder blade and kept traveling until it found a place to fly out just above his left shoulder joint. It stung and the blood was warm as it flowed down his back and settled in his saddle. He couldn't make a stand in that condition. He'd just have to ride on as fast as he could and hope he found a town. A town would mean a doctor, and maybe it would scare them off for a little while. If he lived. All they had to do right now was follow the blood trail. If the wound didn't finish him off, they'd do it without batting an eye. Blue Ridge was only a couple of days away but it might as well be a million miles.

He hugged the horse tighter. There was a small church just ahead of him. He could see the steeple. That meant a town. "Lord," he prayed silently, "help me find a doctor. I don't deserve for you to listen to me after what I've done in my past, but I'll make it right somehow if You can see fit to help me."

The wooden sign outside of town said, "Dodsworth. Pop. 120." He didn't care if the town had a thousand people or barely a dozen or if they'd counted all the dogs hiding under the front porches when they came up with a number for the sign. If it had a doctor with a little magic in his hands, then he'd be happy . . . and maybe alive when morning came.

They were following a hundred yards back when he rode down the main street of town. He passed a general store on the left but there was no shingle for a doctor. He blinked several times and tried to will a small sign into the window

but there was none. Surely there was a doctor in tow, but
which house was the doctor's place? Suddenly, he couldn't
make out anything for the blur in his eyes. He shook his
head and willed himself not to pass out, but still he couldn't
see a single sign swinging from the porch post of a house.
He shut his eyes for just a moment and almost fell off the
horse. He snapped them open and chose a house on the
south side of town. The last house in town. He'd either
have to stop and beg help or ride on, taking his chances
with the bandits behind him. Maybe whoever was inside
could at least send for a doctor.

His foot hung in the stirrup when he tried to dismount
but he finally got it untangled. He grabbed the heavy saddlebags with the gold inside and dragged them across the
small lawn to the porch. The pain in his shoulders was
enough to nauseate him. A fine bead of sweat gathered on
his upper lip but he kept dragging his money. They'd have
to take it away from him if they were going to get it. Everything faded in and out. One minute the house was in focus;
the next, it was a waving mirage like an oasis on the desert.
The lights were still on so whoever lived there hadn't gone
to bed. All he had to do was knock on the door. The saddle
bags made a thud on the wooden porch but not as much of
a thump as he did when all six feet two inches of muscular
man fell in a heap of bloody bones in front of the door.
The last thing he remembered as his life flashed through
his mind was a woman with light gray eyes who trusted
him once upon a time and he'd betrayed that trust. God
surely wouldn't let him into Heaven for his cruelty. As the
darkness wrapped around him, he hoped the men who
would kick his dead body away from the saddle bags un-
derneath him didn't hurt the people inside the house.

The golden light flickering out of the window blinked
only once before darkness swallowed it up. He didn't know
if God heard his prayer, if the people inside blew out the

coal oil lamp, or if the men following him shot the light out. Darkness. Then a bright white light down a tunnel like a coal mine with someone in a white robe beckoning to him on the other end.

Chapter Two

V iolet stuck the crochet hook in the ball of number ten
thread and wrapped the pocket around the whole thing. She
rubbed her eyes and stretched as she stood up. The first
thump on her porch shook the house. The second one was
a little less severe. For a moment she wondered if there'd
been a slight earthquake. She strained her ears and readied
herself for the next shock and heard the snort of a tired
horse. Good grief, Emma's time had come for the baby,
and Jed was out there. She ran to the door, but it wasn't
Jed on her front porch. She opened the door to find a man
lying on her porch. A horse, wet with lather and snorting
with its head down, looked like it couldn't go another step.
Four more horsemen rode by slowly, staring at her every
move. Riding black horses and in all their black attire, their
ominous shadows blocking the stars as they kept moving.

Some drunk had fallen off his horse and crawled up on
her porch. She had a notion to draw back her foot and kick
him right out in the yard, then kick him a couple of more

times until he was in the middle of the street. He could wake up in the morning with a hangover and dust up his nose. She snarled her nose, expecting any minute to get a full whiff of cheap whiskey. His four fine friends had deserted him in his inebriated state but he would have been far better off with them than with her, she'd guarantee that. Hoping to wake him enough so he could stagger away she reached down to shake the fool. When she touched his shoulder something sticky stuck to her palm and she brought back a bloody hand.

"Good grief," she muttered and reached down to grab him under the arms to pull him inside the house. Before she got the door shut, a horseman came tearing up to her house in a dead run. If it was one of those four fools dressed like the devil's henchmen and trying to do this poor man more harm, they'd better come prepared for a tongue lashing, she thought as she took her sewing scissors and cut the shirt from his back.

Jed Thomas stopped his horse on a dime and ran into the house yelling, "It's time, Violet. It's time. I'm going for the doctor."

"Well, you better hurry up," she said. "When the doctor gets done getting you a baby, tell him to stop by here. I've got some poor fool who's been shot or stabbed. Dropped on my porch. Got a death grip on those saddle bags. I'll do what I can until the doctor gets here. Now ride, Jed. It's seven miles there and seven back. Emma might have that baby by herself before you get back if you don't get on."

"But the fellow?" Jed worried.

"He'll either live or die. We don't know him from Cooter's owl. Emma needs some help. It's her first one. Go!" Violet pointed out the door and Jed obeyed.

"Whoever you are, you got a nasty gunshot wound!" She talked as she peeled the remnants of his shirt back. "Whew. Entry hole right here. Tore up the flesh as it went across.

Exit right here. Well, it's a good thing you're asleep, Mister, cause this next thing is going to hurt like the devil."

She left him sprawled out on her living room floor while she went to find the pint of whiskey Zeb left in the house last time he had been home. He'd come in with a chest cold and they'd made a hot toddy. It didn't work. He went out on the next train run and was dead of pneumonia before she saw him again. She opened the bottle and held it over the man's back, slowly pouring it across the raw flesh. He shivered and buried his head even deeper into the crook of his arm.

"Hurts, don't it?" She said. One thing for sure, if he hadn't smelled like a drunk when he got there, he did now. She found clean rags in her sewing remnants and carefully bandaged the wound. Blood seeped through the white batiste fabric but that would have to do until the doctor came. Since the baby was Emma's first and they usually took their own sweet time, that could be after the sun came up on Monday morning. Violet didn't have any notion of trying to move a man that big. He'd be more comfortable in her guest room on the bed, and Violet was a big woman, but not big enough to manhandle all that much dead weight. She tried to pull the saddle bags from him, but he tightened his grip even in unconsciousness so she left them alone.

She sat down in the rocking chair to catch her breath, wondering what she could do next. His pants were a bloody mess, but she wasn't about to take them off. Talk was going to be rampant now. A widow woman with a man in her house all night. Even if he was almost dead there'd still be those who swore it wasn't proper. She heard the horse snort again while she stared at the muscled back of the man.

"Mercy," she muttered. "That poor horse will die out there if I don't take care of him. You aren't going anywhere, Mister," she said, stepping over him.

The horse was still standing where she'd seen him an hour before. He was a big, black fellow with lather drying on his coat. She talked calmly to him as she led him to the stables behind her house, unsaddled him, gave him a drink of cool water and a bag of oats, and commenced to rub him down. He'd need a couple of days of care before he would be able to run again, but that was fine. The man in the house would need more than a couple of days of nursing. He'd need weeks before he could use his arms again without crying out in pain.

The man moaned a few times but never moved his arm from his face in the hours she sat in the rocker and waited for the doctor. It was well past midnight when she heard the buggy approaching from the direction of Jed's farm. She stepped out on the porch and watched the doctor grab his black bag. His shirt sleeves were still rolled up to his elbows and even in the moonlight she could tell he was tired.

"Hear we got a wounded man. Jed said something about him falling on your porch. Let's take a look," he said.

"Is Emma okay? The baby?" Violet held the door open for the doctor.

"Emma is fine. She about had the job done when I got there. Baby is a big girl. And I mean big. About ten pounds worth. Jed is ten feet tall and bullet proof right now. Thinks he just plumb invented fatherhood. Now let's see." His knees creaked when he kneeled on the floor beside the man. He peeled back the bandage and asked Violet to hold the lamp a little closer. "Cleaned it with whiskey. He's a lucky fellow. Lost a lot of blood. It went in here." He pointed at the little round hole in the man's shoulder. "And it furrowed across here and exited over here. Looks like one of them new high-powered rifles and a .22 long bullet. You know they're making them with 40 grains of lead and a hollow point with gilding. Articles I've read says they're the most accurate and popular thing these days. Now, I could be wrong. Doesn't really matter what it was, man's got to get well now. And every time he flexes his fingers, he's going to hurt like the dickens. Guess we'd better get him to bed, Violet. Think you can take care of his feet?"

"Folks is going to talk," she said.

"Folks talk no matter what. He won't stand a ride to Guthrie in this condition. He fell on your porch. Reckon the Good Lord intended for you to take care of him. I'll ride out in a few days to check on him. But you can do as much as I can. Let's put a fresh bandage on him." The doctor opened his bag and brought out a tin of ointment, which he applied lavishly. "Keep this and change that bandage once a day. Clean the wound real good with soap and water. I don't care if he carries on like a wounded mountain lion when the soap hits it. Keep it clean. Use this stuff to keep the bandage from sticking and to help heal the mess. And don't worry about what folks think. It's what you know that matters, Violet. Not what they think. Now you get his feet. Thank goodness he's out of it 'cause there isn't any way to get him in the bedroom without me getting hold of his arms."

The man hugged the saddlebags like they were his lifeline to eternity but finally the doctor wrenched them from his hands and kicked them to one side. Between the Doc and Violet and a lot of heaving they finally got the man into Violet's spare bedroom and on the bed. The man really cried out when they laid him on his back.

"Guess we'd better let him rest on his stomach. That would hurt pretty bad. Get me a basin of water and I'll get him cleaned up. Looks like he bled down into his trousers. Got anything loose fittin' he might wear on his bottom half? Don't want him wearing anything on the top the next few days anyway."

"Got a pair of Zeb's soft pajama bottoms," she said, already on the way out of the room. She dipped enough warm water from the reservoir on her cook stove to fill a basin, tossed in a wash cloth and picked up a bar of lye soap she'd made recently. The doctor had removed the man's boots and socks and was working on his trousers when she set the basin on the stand beside the bed.

She found the pajama bottoms in a trunk at the foot of her bed with the rest of Zeb's clothing. He'd loved his pajamas. Most nights he slept in a berth on the train while the night engineer ran the engines and he was too modest to sleep without anything on or even in his short alls. He wanted real pajamas and he liked soft cotton so she'd sewed them for him. She wasn't sure she wanted another man to wear her dead husband's clothing, but she had about as much choice in that matter as she had in the man falling on her porch.

She knocked on the door, and the doctor called out that she could just put the pants on the door knob. She did and then slumped down in her rocking chair again. Lord, it was going to be morning before she got a moment's sleep. The whole evening began to wear on her. First Jim's wanting to court her. By his declaration, he'd alienated every other eligible bachelor in Logan County from even trying. Not that there were that many who'd be interested in a tall, long in the tooth widow woman anyway. Especially one that was twenty-six years old. Most of the men were looking at the young girls. Women who'd give them lots of children and were a lot more pleasing to the eye than a big horse of a woman who had an independent streak. Maybe she should just tell Jim she was ready for that trip to the bank of the river with a picnic. Or else face up to the fact that she would live without companionship for the rest of her life and die an old widow woman.

She leaned her head on the back of the rocking chair. Jim would probably pitch a fit when he found out that she was harboring a strange man. She chuckled. Nervousness. Weariness. It might be worth keeping the man around just to see if Jim Parsons did have another speed other than slow and stop. She couldn't imagine Jim raising his voice or arguing.

"Well, that's done." Dr. Jones came out of the bedroom, leaving the door wide open. "You're going to need to leave your door open so you can hear him if he tries to get up. Be better to prevent a problem than you try to gather him up and put him back to bed. He might wake up and think he can jump right up and get on down the road. You think you can manage him?"

"I reckon if I can't, I'll get me a chunk of stove wood to help me," Violet said.

"That's the spirit. Now come in here a minute," he said, leading the way back into the room. "The bleeding has stopped but . . ."

"Oh, my!" Violet gasped. "Oh, no!"

"What?" Dr. Jones turned to look at her and thought for a moment he was going to have to pick her up off the hardwood floor. Her face was the color of cold ashes and her gray eyes were widened out with fear, or anger, or maybe both.

"Nothing," she mumbled.

"No, Violet. What's wrong?" He demanded.

"I know that man. His name is Orrin Wilde. We grew up together in Blue Ridge, Texas," she said, barely above a whisper.

"Well, then, it should make caring for him easier. Want me to help you drag those saddle bags in here? Seems like whatever is in them is almighty important to him," Dr. Jones said.

She closed her eyes and wondered what in the world she'd done in her lifetime to deserve punishment like this. But she didn't say a word to the doctor, merely followed him into the living room and bent down to unfasten the buckles from the bags. She gasped when she realized how much gold was inside them. Enough to buy the whole state of Texas, she figured as she dug to the bottom and there was nothing but neat little bags of gold.

"Looks like he's a wealthy man and a dumb one for

carrying this much around with him." Dr. Jones shook his head. "What do you think we'd better do with all this, Violet?"

"You take it to Guthrie. Put it in the bank in his name. That's Orrin with two R's and Wilde with an E at the end. Tell Alford to weigh it up and give you a deposit slip for it. I'll pick it up on Thursday when I come into town. He went to California from Blue Ridge several years ago to work an old gold mine his uncle left to him. Just take it to the bank, please, Doc. That way at least it will be safe. Lord, Almighty, I don't want that much gold anywhere on this place. I bet that's what those four men were after. Would you go by the dressmakers and tell her I won't be in on Tuesday this week?" Violet said.

"What four men?" Dr. Jones drew his eyebrows down in a frown.

"The four who rode past when he was layin' out there on the porch. They looked at me real mean and kept riding. They're probably the ones who shot him and were trying to rob him," she said.

"Most likely. You watch your back, Violet. Men like that won't stop until they get what they want." Dr. Jones wrestled the heavy bags into the buggy. "I'll tell Alford what to do. He'll be at the bank by the time I get into town. Orrin Wilde. Two R's and an E at the end of Wild. Oh, by the way, Alford and Anna Marie are expecting their second now. That first little boy is making Anna Marie pay for her raising."

"Good. I hope the interest is high." Violet managed a weak smile. "And Doc, you watch your back, too. Who's to say those bandits aren't somewhere watching this house and saw you load those bags in your buggy?"

"I'll do it," he said, nodding. "Take care of Mr. Wilde. And if you don't want to make the trip to the dressmakers on Thursday, I'll be out this way to check on him and the new baby. I'll take your sewing back in for you then."

"Thanks," she said, nodding. Sewing was the least of her worries right now. Orrin Wilde was in her spare bedroom, wearing her husband's pajamas, and needing her care. She'd rather be nursing a mean grizzly bear back to health. A little voice chided her conscience, saying, "You prayed for something to make your eyes twinkle. Orrin Wilde sure did that when you were a young woman in Blue Ridge, Texas."

"But I didn't want it to be Orrin Wilde. And I darn sure didn't want him to fall out of Heaven and onto my stoop!" She argued as she locked the front door, blew out the lamp, and stretched out on the settee for the rest of the night. "Not Orrin Wilde. Not him. I would have never prayed for him to even ride past my house again. I never wanted to set eyes on that rascal again as long as I lived. And now he's in my house probably ruining my reputation just like he did eight years ago."

Chapter Three

She pulled her rocking chair into the bedroom at the break of dawn and watched Orrin sleeping soundly. He'd changed little in eight years. Still rakishly handsome with all that dark hair. Heavy lashes rested on his cheeks, but if he opened his eyes they'd be a rich twinkling brown. He'd been a bit lanky back in Blue Ridge but that had filled out nicely. His back lay in ripples of muscles. She didn't remember all that hair back when they were both eighteen, but then she'd never seen Orrin without a shirt on, either.

She remembered other things about Orrin Wilde. Too many other things. She looked away from his sleeping, wounded body, hoping that once he wasn't in her sight the flood of memories would ebb. They didn't. She nervously brushed the skirt of her dress and noticed his blood stains smudged in several places on her best gray Sunday dress. Ignoring what Dr. Jones said about leaving her bedroom door open, she shut it all but a slim crack and dropped her wrinkled, soiled dress on the floor. Next came the petticoats, the camisole, and finally the drawers. She dipped a washcloth in the cold water in the wash basin and swished it around. She wrung the water out of it and applied it to her face. The coolness of the water opened her eyes and relieved the tiredness as well as the confusion.

She slipped into a fresh camisole after washing her aching body. She'd just finished putting on the rest of her clothing and combing her hair neatly when someone knocked on her door. No doubt, it was the first of the folks who'd like to run her out of town on a rail after they'd tarred and feathered her. A strange man had just spent the night with the widow McDonald. Forget that he couldn't raise either arm to compromise her or that he wasn't a stranger. That didn't matter. What did was that her reputation as a respectable widow had just flown out the back door.

She opened the door to find a grinning Jed on the other side. "Mornin'," he said. "I had to run in to the general store for a few things for Emma and thought I'd stop by and tell you the baby is a girl."

"Well, come right in and I'll make us a cup of coffee," she said.

"Can't stay that long. Just wanted to run by. I promised Emma I would. We named her Lalie Joy. After Emma's stepmother, Eulalie, and my sister, Joy. The kids are all excited and Emma's already carryin' on about getting up and making supper tonight," Jed said.

"You tell Emma that she's to stay abed for a few days. Folks used to insist on ten days, but I think that's a bit much. Takes too long to get over the weakness of the bed. But a couple or three and then take it easy," Violet told him.

"I'll tell her but you know Emma. Oh, what happened with that fellow that was shot up or stabbed?" Jed turned at the edge of the porch.

"He's in my spare room. Doc Jones says he can't be

moved. Turned out to be a fellow I knew down in Blue Ridge, Texas. We grew up together. Name is Orrin Wilde. He hasn't come to yet, but then he lost a lot of blood," Violet said.

"Well, he'll be all right with you to look after him," Jed said.

"Reckon people will talk?" Violet raised an eyebrow.

"People always talk, that's the way of it. But those of us who know you trust you. Come out and see the baby soon as your boarder gets where you can leave him for a few hours," Jed said and was gone.

"My boarder," she said, shaking her head.

She'd no more than finished her breakfast when someone else tramped across her wooden porch and knocked heavily on the door. She found Jim on the other side, his hat in his hand and a concerned look on his face. "Hello, what brings you to this end of the street?" she asked.

"Heard you had a man who slept here last night. I think me and you need to talk," he said.

"Well, come on in, Jim," she said, holding the door open for him. The gossip vine had surely sprouted quickly that morning. Maybe it was an answer to a prayer after all. She'd wondered how she was going to handle the situation she found herself in with Jim Parsons. Perhaps it had just worked itself out. "Can I get you a glass of water or a cup of coffee?"

"No, Violet. I didn't come here to socialize with you. I come to speak my piece and then I'll go. I been admirin' you for a long time. Since before Zeb died, I thought I'd like to have a woman like you. Steady, you know. Not flighty like Anna Marie or the young women her age. But a helpmate like you. Then Zeb up and died off on one of those trips with the pneumonia, and I've waited the year what was proper. But I ain't going to be the laughing stock of Dodsworth, Violet. I'll still court you proper for six months and then marry up with you, but that man in there has got to go today. I understand you didn't have no other choice last night since he just fell on your doorstep, but you can hire a wagon to take him to Guthrie to the hotel. So that's my piece. If he don't go then I ain't goin' to be comin' around here courting you. I'll be good to you. Make you a good husband. Won't put too many demands on you. You'll just have to quit that sewing business for the woman over in Guthrie because I don't cotton to the idea of a wife working. And you'll have to get rid of that man. It ain't fittin' and I won't stand for it. Now is he going?" Jim asked.

It was more words than Violet had heard out of the man in two years, even if was a straight-up monologue. He'd just as well have been visiting with her about buying a dependable horse as talking about courting her. "Well, Jim, it's like this. Dr. Jones says the fellow can't be moved for a long time so I've got to care for him. Got no other choice. I guess that makes it pretty plain. He can't be moved. You can't live with that. I suppose maybe you better just go on and find someone else to court. You ever think about Maggie?"

"Maggie Listen ain't wife material," he said, curtly. "Well, you made your choice whether you had a choice in it or not. You could move him if you was interested in my attentions, but you don't see it that way. So I won't be offering to drive you home from church on Sunday no more. And we won't be goin' on that picnic to the creek, neither. I don't hold grudges so I'll speak to you when we meet on the street, but anything else is finished, Violet," he said.

"I understand." She followed him to the door and leaned against the jamb as he drove away without looking back. "Three men in my life and all of them left," she said. She picked up the broom and began sweeping out the house, wishing all the time that she could sweep the memories from her heart and mind. Zeb would have been like Jim.

If he'd come home from the train on Tuesday and found Orrin in the spare room, he would have told her the same thing Jim did. Get him out. Don't matter if the man dies on the way to Guthrie. It ain't fitting. But Zeb was dead and had been for a year.

She attacked the floor with the broom as if by sweeping away every speck of dust and dirt, she would solve all the problems in her heart. By the middle of the afternoon, a fine bead of anger had boiled up from the middle of her chest. She hadn't asked for a bit of this mess. She didn't ask for the reputation she got back in Blue Ridge when she was barely eighteen. She didn't ask for Zeb to up and die of pneumonia. And even if she did utter a prayer about someone coming into her life, she sure didn't mention Orrin Wilde's name or even conjure up a vision of his handsome face during her short prayer either. Time was when she would have supplied the bullet for those four rascals to shoot him, and baked them a chocolate layer cake if they'd hit him right in the heart. She picked up a dust rag and obliterated every speck from the living room. Still she could easily have chewed up railroad spikes and spit out ten penny nails.

It wasn't a good time for Anna Marie to come visiting, but she did.

Anna Marie took a seat on the edge of a chair in the living room without even being asked in or to sit down. "Violet, honey, surely you've got some good cold tea we could sip on while we visit," she said.

"As a matter of fact, I don't," Violet said. Mercy, she'd never been rude to anyone in her life. Not even when Anna Marie was trying to break up Emma and Jed's marriage. "But I can offer you a glass of water," she said, attempting to mend her hateful attitude.

"No, I wanted tea and nothing else will cure my craving. You know of course that Alford and I are going to be blessed again in a few months. Little Al wants a baby brother but I think a daughter might be nice." Anna Marie fanned her pretty face with the back of her hand. "Momma says you got a man living with you. He just fell right out of the sky on your porch step last night. That's really why I come to see you today, Violet. You know it ain't right for a man to be sleeping here with you."

"Well, Anna Marie, since I'm a few years older than you and since it's my house, I expect what I do in it is my business. However, that man in there in my spare bedroom is scarcely able to lift his arms or compromise me in any way. He certainly is not sleeping with me as you put it. He's wounded bad enough that the doctor says he can't be moved for a while. A long while. So I suppose if that's going to ruin my widow's spotless reputation, then that's just how it'll have to be." Violet sat down in her rocker and picked up her crochet. Her hands were so clammy that the thread didn't want to feed around her little finger and across the hook, but she wouldn't lay it down. She'd be hanged if Anna Marie got the impression she was nervous.

"I just came to tell you for your own good, Violet. Folks is already talking. Some folks say you knew the man down in Texas before the land run. They're saying he knew whose porch he was coming to and that you was waiting on him to get here. Just that you didn't know he was going to be shot up. Poor old Jim has waited a whole year to do what was right by you and you've just plumb broke his heart. You know he's a good catch. Good dependable man. You being so old and so tall and ugly, why he's probably the best you could ever hope for," Anna Marie said, sniffing loudly as she stuck her nose dramatically in the air.

"If Jim Parsons is such a good catch then why did you marry Alford? Looks to me like you would have been flirting with him?" Violet asked.

"Jim Parsons is just too plain and old for me, Violet. Mercy, just the thought of me with him is enough to make me giggle. But you're a widow. You can't take your pick like I could. And besides, you're old." Anna Marie shrugged her shoulders.

"I guess twenty-six would be old to you, but let me tell you Anna Marie, it's not so old when you are that age. And what goes on between me and Jim Parsons isn't your business, either. I don't have to explain one thing to you. Whether I knew Orrin Wilde or not has nothing to do with the fact that he's staying right here until he's able to leave. That's the doctor's orders and I'm not having a dead man on my conscience just so I could save what you thought my reputation ought to be," Violet said.

"Don't get huffy with me, Violet McDonald," Anna Marie snapped. She stood up abruptly and crossed the floor to stare in the bedroom where Orrin slept fitfully. "Oh, my, and he's undressed on the top half. How could you allow such a thing, Violet? Besides, he's too handsome to ever fall for you if that's what you've got in mind. Get him well and then he'll marry you out of respect for what he's stolen from you? Well, it won't work with that one. He's too good looking to ever let a tall horsy woman like you in his life."

"Kind of like Emma is too tall for Jed?" Violet said, knowing fully well she was delivering barb for barb and unable to tame her tongue one whit.

"Whatever poor old Jed saw in that big raw-boned woman will always be a mystery to me when he could have had me. But that's water under the bridge and hasn't got a thing to do with this man in your bed. Just don't expect the women in Dodsworth to be nice to you. I'm leaving now. I've got to be back in Guthrie by the time Alford gets off work. And besides, little Al drives Momma crazy if I leave him there more than a little while. I just wanted to use my time to try to convince you to do what's right, is all. Now that I've spoken my piece, you can do whatever you like. Just be careful, Violet McDonald. Your good name is on the line, here," she said and was out the door before Violet could answer.

"If anyone else speaks their piece today I may kick them out into the street," she said aloud as she opened a jar of soup and put it in a pot to boil. She checked on Orrin, then went out to the spring house and carried in a nice big chunk of venison that Jed had brought the day when he and the family came to church. It would give the soup a rich broth, and Orrin needed good food to keep his resistance up.

She stirred up a batch of fresh yeast bread and set it to rise on the warmer shelf of the stove. Good sturdy soup and bread would heal any body. Too bad it wouldn't heal a broken heart and a crushed soul.

Orrin heard voices somewhere out there and clutched the pillow under his head even tighter. His back ached. The sorry rascals must have hit him with that last shot and left him to die. He tried to open an eye but it wouldn't cooperate. Maybe he was dead and had gone on to eternity. He breathed in a lung full of the smell of sheets dried in the fresh air. Maybe he'd made it all the way to Blue Ridge and was sleeping in one of his mother's beds. He drifted in and out of semi-consciousness all morning. He heard someone sweeping the floor. The swish of the broom and something else. Something he'd forgotten these past eight years. The rustling of a woman's skirt tails. Then he dropped back into that gray area where he didn't know whether he'd died or was still living.

Sometime in the middle of the afternoon two women argued about something. He could hear the tone of their voices and the cutting edge to their words. Did women argue in the hereafter as well as on earth? If they did, eternity couldn't be that wonderful, stress-free place men preached it up to be. He lost that train of thought as quickly as the others he'd struggled with throughout the day. Some other time, gentle hands removed something from his back and put a soothing salve on his wound. She fussed at him when he moaned, and the voice sounded familiar, but he couldn't keep his thought pattern in a straight line long enough to figure out who it was.

"Okay Orrin Wilde, I didn't choose this for my lot, but you're going to wake up now and eat some soup. Even a few bites will build up your strength," Violet said in a no-nonsense voice.

Orrin tried to open his eyes. He really did. That sounded like Violet Daniels telling him the what-for about eating soup. He must have caught fever in the gunshot wound. Was it last night or a week ago? Whenever it was, he'd lain for days until someone found him and now he was delirious. It couldn't be Violet. Not his Violet.

"I said open your eyes," she demanded.

They both popped open ever so briefly before he shut them against the blinding light of day. All that blistering light made his eyes hurt as bad as his back. He squeezed them tightly and then relaxed the eyelids. He'd open one eye only a slit to see who was talking to him. He smelled soup, real, honest to goodness soup. And was that home-made bread? He would shoot his best friend for a loaf of homemade bread, but he couldn't make himself open his eyes.

"Orrin Wilde," she said.

He managed to get one eye open enough to see a tall woman sitting in a rocking chair right beside his bed. A feather bed with sheets and a pillow. Luxury deluxe. The lady wore a light blue dress and had dark hair. Sunlight streamed through the window, lighting up her face, and he thought he was looking at an angel when he managed to get both eyes open.

"Well, that's a step in the right direction. Now we're going to ease you up gently and sit you up in this bed. There is no way you can eat laying flat on your stomach. It's going to hurt. But if you go at it easy, maybe it won't break loose and bleed," she said. She turned him as carefully as she could until he was on his side, then helped him to sit up. He weaved like he was about to fall out of the bed and she steadied him with a hand around his waist until he got control. Then she propped big pillows all around him, making a nest so he could sit without falling. Using a pillow like the arm of a chair, she propped one hand, noticing that he winced at even that much arm movement. She was as careful . . . even if she would like to have been holding the gun that shot him. Except, if she'd been aiming, he wouldn't be here making faces at the pain. He'd already be discussing his future with Saint Peter.

"Now, you are going to open your mouth, and I'm going to feed you," she said, desperately trying to keep the breathlessness from her voice. Just touching his hand brought back a whole bevy of memories she thought she'd long since forgotten. And knowing that Orrin still had that effect on her sure didn't do anything to calm her antsy anger, either.

"Is that you, Violet Daniels?" he asked hoarsely around a dry mouth.

"It's me, Orrin Wilde. You fell right on my porch last night. Open your mouth," she said, starting toward his face with a spoon full of soup.

He opened his mouth and held the soup inside for a long time before he began to chew. Even the simple job of chewing shot needles of pain into his shoulders, but it tasted so good. When the next bite left the bowl, he had his mouth open like a baby bird, waiting for it to be filled.

"Did I die?" he asked when he'd swallowed.

"No, Orrin, you didn't, but I expect you'll wish you had before you're well enough to leave this house," she said.

Chapter Four

"**I**'m not layin' in this bed another day. It's the most humiliating thing I've ever had to do, Violet. Depending on you for every single thing." Orrin slung his legs off the edge of the bed and stood up, a bit wobbly but at least he was on his feet. A man could lay down and die or he could rise up and get on with life. Orrin had lain abed for three days and it was time for him to get up.

"Well, that's poetic justice," she snapped. "Don't you even mention humiliation to me, Orrin."

"You sure are a sassy piece of baggage. Strange, I don't remember you being that way in Blue Ridge," he said, testing his strength by taking one step toward her. *Lord*, he prayed desperately if silently, *please don't let me fall right at her feet.*

"What happened in Blue Ridge is over. We're two different people now, Orrin. You better be careful. You go to fall and catch with those arms and you'll tear all the mending up in your shoulders." She stepped back and let him through the doorway into the living room.

31

He was sweating bullets by the time he walked across the floor and settled down gently into the first chair. So much for all those plans about how he'd just hop right up, saddle up his horse and ride on home to Blue Ridge. Those varmints who shot him had really done a number on his back, and all the blood he'd lost really had weakened his body, whether his mind wanted to admit it or not. "Why didn't you tell me it was a hundred miles from that bed to this rocking chair?" he asked.

She settled herself on the settee and picked up a sleeve to do a bit of fancy work around the edge. She sat ramrod straight, her back barely touching the settee, and didn't answer him. She wouldn't let a puppy die and a man's life was worth a lot more than a dog's, but that didn't mean she had to socialize with Orrin. Not even after eight years, and especially not after that business in Blue Ridge.

"Are you going to answer me?" he persisted.

"No," she said.

"What happened after I left town?" he asked.

She ignored him and kept crocheting. If he asked her to help him get back to the bed she'd do it. If he asked when supper was, she'd tell him. But Violet Daniels McDonald didn't intend to do much past that. According to Anna Marie she was already compromising her position in the community as it was—but that wasn't the reason Violet was being so obstinate.

She'd lived in Blue Ridge, Texas, her whole entire life. Been born there. Went to school. Fell in love. It had been a storybook life until Orrin Wilde pulled his stunt. And then she'd been the object of secret whispers in Blue Ridge.

"Violet, we can't stay in the same house until I get well and not even have adult conversation," he said, snappishly.

"Want to bet?" She dropped the sewing in her lap and looked him right in the eyes. Zeb's pajamas hung on his slim hips and stopped an inch above his ankle bone. His feet were long and narrow; his chest, covered these days by the pajama top, was broad and muscular. Three days in bed had not taken any kind of toll on the muscles in his upper arms. He looked like he could break a railroad tie in two without taxing his strength.

However, until the gash all the way from one shoulder blade to the other healed, his arms were practically useless. Overuse would break open the wound which had started healing nicely. He was a lucky man that infection hadn't brought on fevers. "I don't have to talk to you Orrin. I talked to you the last night I saw you until I was blue in the face. I thought we had it all settled that night, but we didn't. So why should I talk to you now? Give me two good reasons."

Because I've never stopped loving you. Not even in eight years. Because I want to talk to you. I want to know you again. Are those reasons enough? That's what he thought, but he didn't say that at all. "Guess I made a mess of things, didn't I? I just wanted an adventure. I thought if we went to California we could make our fortune and come home then. Buy a parcel of land and own it. Farm a little. Raise a few cows. Why couldn't you just trust me? Evidently you went on your own adventure later because otherwise you wouldn't be here."

The question jerked her up short. She'd thought when she left Blue Ridge two years before that she'd never face all that again. But here it was, right in her lap for the second time. Whispers behind her back. For the second time in her life, she was the object of gossip. She didn't like it the first time and she didn't like it a bit better the second time. The fight had been eight years in coming but it was there before them now, and they might as well get it over with. There might not be a house when they got finished. She might saddle up his horse for him, put him on it, and then catch the next train to anywhere in the world but Dodsworth or Blue Ridge, Texas.

"I did trust you. I trusted you to be at the church the

next day. Do you have any idea how I felt standing there on my father's arm waiting for you to come in the side door with the preacher? Finally the preacher stuck his head in the door and motioned for my father. You were gone. Gone, Orrin." She raised her voice and her gray eyes shot daggers at him. "My father tried to be calm about the whole thing. Simply told the congregation that you weren't coming to the wedding because you'd had a change of heart. They all went home. Don't you ever talk to me about humiliation because you won't ever know how I felt, standing there in my white dress with roses in my hair and a bouquet all tied up with a white satin ribbon. Momma took me by the arm and begged me to go home with her and Daddy, but I didn't, Orrin. I stayed from that morning until after dark. I sat on the front pew and waited for you for hours, then I kneeled at the altar and prayed for hours. God either didn't hear my prayers or He said no. I just knew you'd realize that you loved me enough to give up your hare-brained adventure. I kept telling myself that over and over. But you didn't come back. I walked three miles home in a blinding rainstorm. When I got there I took the wedding cake out in the front yard and fed it to the hounds. Didn't seem quite right to eat it."

"I'm sorry," he said.

"You bet your sorry scraggly rear end, you're sorry. Only a sorry human being would do that to another one, and you'd professed to love me for four years, Orrin. When you love someone you don't treat them like that," she said, stoically.

"But I begged you, Violet. I wasn't lying when I said I loved you. But we were both just eighteen. We had our whole life in front of us to make a home and have a family. I wanted you to go with me. Why did you come to the land run when you wouldn't go with me to the gold mine my uncle left to me?" His eyes danced with as much anger as she had in hers.

"When you left folks talked." She smoothed the front of her dress and sat back, settling into the settee more comfortably. "They said all kinds of cruel things. I had a reputation then. You were running away from a wanton hussy of some kind. They said I must have something wrong with me and you saw the light just before it was too late. In a few weeks, women scarcely would even speak to me. Then Zeb McDonald came to visit me. He said he was working for the railroad and he'd marry me. I told him I didn't love him and he said a marriage didn't have to be a love arrangement. He needed a wife and I needed a proper name again. So we went to the preacher and he married us that day. There was some that said I'd been seeing Zeb on the sly and that your heart was broke and you ran away because of that. Six years went by and Zeb wanted to claim a piece of land with the land run. By then I didn't care where I lived, so I agreed. He was able to get some acreage over by where Jed and Emma live, but he worked the railroad five days a week. He had some men build me this house in town, and I've lived here ever since. We planned on building a house out there in the country. Improving the land so we could get a clear title to it." Her voice trailed off. The fight had been anticlimactic after all. Nothing worth fighting for after all those years. Too much water under the bridge, as the old saying went. Orrin Wilde and Violet Daniels had had their time, but it had long since passed.

"I can't believe you married Zeb McDonald," he said, raising his voice to just an octave below screaming. The veins in his neck were tight, pulsating cords and his face turned scarlet with pent-up rage seeking a vent.

"Believe it, honey. I married him. Stood right up there in front of the altar where you forsook me and promised to love, honor, and obey him until death parted us," she screamed right back at him. So much for their passion dying in its sleep after all those years. They both still had enough fire in them to fight about things after all.

"Zeb? Lord Almighty, Violet, he was ten years older than us and bald. He had to have been nearly thirty. Why did you marry him?" All the wind went out of Orrin's sails. Violet was married and there was no future for them. She'd said Zeb was out on the train for days at a time. That's why he hadn't been home yet. But when he did, Orrin would have to ride out of town whether he could sit a horse or not. Zeb was as straightlaced as an old maid school teacher. Knowing what he did about Orrin, he might just shoot him for even being in his house.

"Because he could give me back what you took with you when you left. Respectability. I wasn't that poor little Daniels girl who got jilted at the altar. There wasn't something dreadful wrong with me and I hadn't committed some horrible sin to make you forsake our vows. Zeb offered me his name and I took it." She wanted to reach across the room and slap his face for even asking such a stupid question.

Orrin set his jaw in fury and jerked his head around to look at something else other than Violet. Anything to tame the rage in his heart and keep the stinging, salty tears from his eyes. Grown men didn't cry. Especially when they were the very ones who had caused the problem to begin with. Zeb had done well by Violet. Her small white frame house was filled with nice furniture. The windows had glass panes covered by frilly white lace curtains. Everywhere he looked he could see Violet's touches. A vase of wildflowers on the mantle above the cold fireplace. Shiny hardwood floors that she kept with vigilance. A beautiful piano. Could she still make music come out of a piano that made a man's feet ache to dance? He remembered Saturday nights when he picked up the fiddle, her folks rolled back the rug, and the whole community gathered to dance. Did she ever remember the way both their hearts raced when they made beautiful music together?

"So when is he coming home?" he asked. Today? To-morrow? When did Orrin have to be well enough to at least throw his saddlebags over the horse and go away. This time he wouldn't be walking away from Violet with near as much spit and vinegar as he'd done eight years before. He'd told himself that day that in a year he'd have enough gold to buy Violet a decent farm. She'd be madder than a wet hen after a tornado when he didn't show up for the wedding, but she'd forgive him when he came home with the money and they'd get married then.

"Who?" Violet asked.

"Zeb. When's he coming home? You said he was out on the train for days at a time. Is he due home soon?" Orrin asked.

"Zeb died of the pneumonia last year. I've been a widow for a year," she said.

Orrin's soul went out to her. She'd surely been through a lot for a woman only twenty-six years old. But his heart wanted to dance a jig right there in the living room floor. She wasn't married anymore.

"I can't believe some fellow hasn't already laid claim to the widow McDonald," he said testily.

"Who says they haven't?" She snapped right back at him. "I'm going to make your lunch, now, Orrin Wilde. We've got to make you well so you can go home to Blue Ridge. Who knows, all the young women there probably don't care that you are a rascal. They won't know that they'd better chain you to the altar on the day before you marry so you'll be there at the right time."

"My, my, aren't you hateful today?" he said.

"I'm just whatever life has made me. And you had a big hand in that, so you can keep your mouth shut." She pointed a finger at him as she went to the kitchen.

He could hear her preparing lunch. She was crazy as old

Sally Simball down in Blue Ridge if she thought the argument was over. It had really just begun and it might never have an end. "So what did Zeb have that I didn't to make you come all the way to Oklahoma and leave your Momma and Daddy?" he yelled over his shoulder.

"You watch your mouth, Orrin." She was right at his shoulder and startled him when she spoke. He'd expected her to yell from the kitchen. "Zeb was a decent, good man. Don't you ever talk about him like that. Momma and Daddy both died with the cholera when me and Zeb had been married two years. There ain't nothing in Blue Ridge for me anymore, Orrin. Brothers and sisters all moved away, and I was the last one home if you'll remember. Your own folks sold out and moved over to Leonard before we come to the land run. So you can go back there without anyone knowing what a skunk you've been."

"If I'm that big of a problem, I'll just go on my merry way. I can go over to Guthrie and get a room at the hotel there. Close to the doctor anyway," he said between gritted teeth.

"Sure you can. Who's going to saddle your horse, honey? And who's going to lift you up and put you on it? I've been called a big horse of a woman before but I'm not going to lift my little finger to help you ride off and die. I've already lost my spotless reputation as a respectable widow, so you're here until you are thoroughly healed." She bent down until her nose was barely inches from his. She'd planted her hands on her hips and she'd raised her voice until she sounded like a fish wife.

"Who called you a horse of a woman?" he asked incredulously. Violet was the most gorgeous woman he'd ever laid eyes on. He'd fallen in love with her in the first grade when she was a head taller than him. It wasn't until they were fourteen that she stopped growing and he caught up and surpassed her height.

"Men! You've all got selective hearing. You only hear

what you want to. Don't you turn the tables on this argument. It doesn't matter who called me that. What matters is that you're not going anywhere, so suck up the idea and shut up about it. You think you're so big and strong, then we'll see how well you do at trying to lift your left arm and feed yourself," she said.

"I can do it, honey," he said, using the same term of endearment as sarcastically as she'd just done. "You just get it ready and I'll sit up to your table and show you just how much Wilde blood I've got in me. I come from sturdy stock, you know."

"You got that right. About Wilde blood." She snorted and disappeared into the kitchen again.

He used the forward motion of the rocking chair to help him get up without putting his hands on the arms and pushing away. For just a minute the room spun around in circles, the piano appeared to tilt to one side, and the flowers on the settee blurred around the edges. But then he got it under control and slowly made his way out to the kitchen. He would be there at the table when lunch was served and she wouldn't see him walking in tiny little shuffling steps like an old man.

She heard the rocking chair stop and leaned back just enough to make sure he wasn't going to fall in a heap of loose connected bones on her rug. It had taken hours of scrubbing to get the blood out of it Monday morning. If he did something totally ignorant like fall on it again, she intended to kick his argumentative, sorry hide right out the front door. He could bleed in the grass just as well as on her good rug. He tottered for a moment, then seemed to right himself and started toward the kitchen. She quietly slipped a chair out away from the table. Crazy man, he would have probably tried to lift it himself, just to keep from humiliating himself further by asking her to do it for him.

She pretended to ignore him but held her breath until he

was seated beside the table. She dished up two bowls of potato soup and took a pan of cornbread from the oven. The iron skillet of bread took center place on the table. She laid silverware before his place and her own, then set the bowls of steamy soup on the table. When she'd scated herself and said grace, she looked across the table at him and waited.

"What?" he demanded.

"Just making sure that Wilde blood is going to stand you in good steed, or if I need to move my chair around there and feed you again today," she said.

"I can do it." His lips became a firm line of determination. He picked up the spoon and dipped it into the soup. He told his arm to take it to his mouth, and it tried really hard; but every inch it raised the spoon was sheer torture to his back. With a bead of sweat across his upper lip, he almost gave up. But if he had to move Heaven and earth and visit with the devil himself about the price of his soul, he intended to get at least one bite to his mouth that day. Bending toward the spoon hurt as bad as making his arm raise upward. But Orrin knew for a fact that if he didn't push himself, he'd lose the use of his arms. Finally the soup was inside his mouth. It tasted really good but his stomach was so queasy from the effort, he had difficulty swallowing.

"Very good," she commented as she effortlessly ate her own lunch. "Want butter on your cornbread, or can you do that, too?"

"Yes, ma'am, I would like a piece of that cornbread very much, and I would appreciate it if you would butter it for me," he said respectfully.

"Hurt like the dickens, didn't it?" she said, as she lathered sweet cream butter on a wedge of golden yellow cornbread.

He was in the process of lifting his spoon to his mouth and only nodded in answer to her question. Even that simple gesture made his shoulders cry in agony. "Yes, it did.

But I'm doing it, Violet. And tonight at supper I'll feed myself. In a few days it won't be such a big chore."

"Good. Then you can be gone," she said. But she didn't look at Orrin when she said that. Because they were just words and didn't come from her heart.

Chapter Five

Dark clouds scuttled toward Dodsworth from the southwest. Violet watched them with interest. Tornadoes came from that direction. Like all folks in Texas and Oklahoma she had a healthy respect for tornadoes, bred in her from a child. What on earth would she do with Orrin if a tornado did hit Dodsworth?

He'd eaten at the table for two days and was doing a fair job of shaving himself even if it did cause him a lot of pain. The holes where the bullet went in and came out were still pretty raw looking, so she could imagine what the inside of the furrow looked like. Dr. Jones had come the day before to check Orrin and said the welt across his back was healing well. He had declared that he'd hire Violet as a nurse any time she wanted to give up sewing.

"Looks a storm brewing. Think I'll walk out to the stables and check on the horses. My big black don't like storms," Orrin said so close to her that she could feel his warm breath on her neck.

"Be careful," she said, willing herself not to shiver. "You haven't been that far yet so you might get tired. Oh, and I fed them before supper, so don't be lifting any oat bags."

"If I get tired I'll sit a spell before I try to get back. And no, ma'am, I will not lift an oat bag," he said with a bright grin that lit up his whole face. In the past few days he'd gotten used to her bossing him around like a child. Sometimes he felt like one with his arms so weak. It was a good thing he'd fallen on Violet's doorstep, because those wicked bandits would have left him to die if they hadn't finished off the job. Without her expert help he would have bled to death. Or infection would have set in, and he would be dead because of that.

He inhaled deeply when he stepped off the back porch. It smelled like rain and felt like hail. The temperature had dropped at least ten degrees since he left the comfort of the front porch and did his slow shuffle through the living room and kitchen to tell her he was going to the stables. He stopped and sniffed again about half way across the yard. Something else was in the air. Not something he could name, but something like the feeling he had that night when the robbers shot him. Danger. He smelled danger. And yet there couldn't be trouble here in Dodsworth. If the rascals who shot him were coming back to finish the job and take his money, they'd have done it before a whole week had passed. No, that wasn't what it was. He shook his head slowly trying to make the feeling go away. He convinced himself that it was simply because he was getting out of the house on his own power for the first time. Going to a man's domain . . . the stables. Seeing his faithful old horse that had carried him all the way to California and back across the land, too. Fear that he might fall or that his horse wouldn't recognize him. Those were the things that brought the uneasiness to his heart.

The stable doors were open. He'd have to remember to fuss at Violet for leaving them open when she went to feed and water the horses. A storm was approaching fast, and she should know better than to leave the doors open. Maybe, just maybe, he'd be able to shut them himself. By using a foot to shove the doors, he wouldn't test his arms or tear the wound open in his back. Then he wouldn't have to say a word to her about the doors. She had enough on her mind taking care of him without having to do a man's work as well. Orrin felt right proud of himself when he walked into the stables and up to the stall where his horse, Coaly, was kept. The horse lowered his head for the petting he knew was forthcoming and Orrin chuckled. Horses— now, they were a man's friend. Women could never be as close to a man as his horse, no matter how long or how hard they tried.

Violet carried the dishpans full of water to the back porch and tossed the water out on the peony plants. Next month they'd be in full bloom. Light pink and white blossoms as big as saucers. She'd have to separate them this fall and divide the tubers. They were getting entirely too crowded in the small area she set aside for them. Maybe Emma would want a starting of them. Or maybe she'd make a flower bed out toward the stables. Thinking of that, she looked around to see just where she might make another peony bed and remembered that she'd shut the stable doors when she saw the storm clouds.

"Darn that man," she fussed. He'd opened the stable doors by himself. She hadn't thought about that when he said he was going to see his horse. She'd even put the bar across when she went out to feed and water the horses. How on earth had he gotten that job done when he still had trouble with simple little jobs taking care of himself? Oh, well, if he came back in the house with blood all over his bandages, then he could just expect her to pitch a hissy fit.

While he was out of the bedroom seemed like an ideal time to go in there and change his linens. She took all the sheets from the bed along with the pillow cases and tossed them in the corner. Then she opened a bureau drawer beside the bed and took out a clean set. Pure, sparkling white and smelling just like the fresh air they'd been dried in. She buried her nose in them for a few seconds. She snapped the first one out over the bed and it landed with precision exactly in the center. She tucked the corners in neatly and proceeded to put the top sheet on. By the time she had the bed finished she was humming. She grabbed the dust mop and gave the hardwood floor a once-over, but she didn't use any oil on the mop. A slick floor could make Orrin fall. She bent at the waist and slid the mop under the bed. It hit the saddlebags she'd put under there the next day when Orrin kept fussing in his sleep about his saddlebags. She'd taken out a camp cooking set—a coffee pot, mug, plate and skillet—along with a couple of changes of clothing. She'd washed the trousers and shirts, along with the short-all undergarments and socks, and folded them neatly. They were in the bureau drawer beneath the sheets. Then she filled the saddlebags with rocks and gravel. That way if he got really agitated and tried to move them they'd be as heavy as if they had real gold in them. When he got well enough to give up Zeb's pajamas, she'd tell him what she did with his gold. He could ride over to Guthrie, take care of his business, and be gone. And that wouldn't be a minute too soon.

When she finished dusting, she kicked the edge of the saddlebags back under the bed. He sure didn't need to try to open them. Lord, he'd have a spell if he did. But they'd given him comfort just knowing they were there and safe, it seemed like. She looked out the back door again. Apparently, he and that horse he called Coaly were having quite a heart-to-heart talk. Either that or he was so glad to be out of her presence that he'd fallen asleep on the loose hay.

She went on into her bedroom and began the same process of changing sheets. That way, they'd be ready for early morning laundry on Monday. She opened the top drawer of her bureau and took out a clean set and repeated the process of making and remaking a bed. It had to be tight enough to bounce a penny on, according to her grandmother Daniels. Violet wasn't sure a woman could get past the first step on the way up to the Pearly Gates if she didn't make up a bed right on Saturday evenings. Washing was done on Monday. Ironing on Tuesday. Baking on Wednesday. House cleaning on Thursday. Friday was for catching up on everything else. Saturday was getting the beds remade so the laundry could be started early on Monday. That made a good wife; one a husband wouldn't ever leave. Too bad Orrin hadn't stayed around to see just how good and tight she could make a bed.

By the time she finished that job, she was sweaty hot. It was too early to drag out the tub and take a real bath. The sun hadn't even set yet, and besides, the water in the reservoir hadn't had time to heat up. So she shut her bedroom door and peeled off her shirt waist, dipped a wash cloth in the cool water in the basin painted with blue roses, and laid it on her bare neck. It felt so good that she pushed the cloth down inside her camisole. Visions of a nice, cool lake like the one in Blue Ridge danced in her head. The one where she and her cousins went swimming when the boys were all off fishing or somewhere where they couldn't see the girls in their undergarments. Emma made Jed's nieces bathing costumes last summer, Violet remembered. She wondered if she and Emma might make themselves such a costume and go swimming this summer.

Orrin thought the pressure in the small of his back was Violet. She'd caught him unawares talking to his horse and was poking at him to make him turn around so she could give him a scalding lecture about being out so long. Especially with storm clouds on the horizon. He was ready to turn around when someone poked him again and he realized it wasn't Violet at all. What he felt was the barrel of a rifle and the man holding it smelled like he hadn't had a bath since last year sometime.

"So you are not dead, amigo?" the man said with a heavy accent.

"I am not dead," Orrin turned very slowly to face four men with four guns trained on various parts of his body.

"We were not sure. We have been watching the house and you did not come out. We are here to take the saddle-bags with the gold in them. Our uncle says you have gotten all of the good gold. He paid you well for the claim, amigo. It will not produce the gold so he will take yours. We will take it to him." The man showed yellowed teeth when he grinned.

"I don't have it anymore," Orrin said. He couldn't take four men like them into the house. They'd kill him anyway when they got the gold, and they'd hurt Violet.

"Ah, I think you are lying to me, amigo. Those bags were under you when you crawled onto the pretty lady's porch. One of us has watched the house ever since the next morning, and the bags have not left there. So you tell us where they are hidden or we will go inside and the pretty lady will tell us. Of course, we may have to . . ." The man let his voice trail off but the meaning was clear.

Orrin was in a worse pickle than he'd ever been before. The bags were under his bed, and there was no way to warn Violet to run from the house. "If I give you the bags, will you ride away with them and not hurt the lady?"

"You have our word of honor, amigo." The man chuckled. "We just want the gold. We aren't interested in the giant woman."

"I'll get them only after if you let me go into the house alone and tell her to ride away before you come inside. That way I'll know she is safe and you aren't going to hurt her," Orrin said.

"We are not stupid men. If we let you go in the house

alone, you can arm yourself and we won't have the gold," he said.

"How could I shoot you? My arms are no good. I can barely feed myself," he said honestly.

"No! That is not the way it is." Another of the men stepped forward and slapped him on the back hard enough that Orrin saw stars and his knees turned to jelly. "We are all going into that house or we will kill you right here. Then we will go inside, find the woman, and after while we will kill her, too. So now you walk, Mr. Wilde, toward that house. If you fall down I'll put a bullet in your heart. That is where I was aiming the night you got shot. I am still mad because I missed. I never waste ammunition."

Orrin began a slow shuffle back toward the house. Something warm and oozy ran down his back and he didn't have to touch it to know it was blood. He prayed that someone would drive by. Perhaps Jed Thomas that Violet talked about. Or even the preacher man coming to gripe at Violet for having a man in her house. Anyone. For any reason. Just someone so he could call out to them to get Violet out of the house.

God did not hear his prayer.

The man with the ugly teeth opened the back door and shoved him inside. When he drew his hand back he had blood on it. He just grinned and wiped it on his pants leg. "Amigo, you take me to the saddlebags and I promise I will not make you bleed anymore."

"You have promised not to hurt the woman," Orrin reminded him.

"And you trusted Damian?" One of the other four cackled. "He's the devil in the flesh. He will lie, steal, or cheat at anything. It is funny that you would trust the devil."

Violet was about to open her bedroom door when she heard a coarse accent say something about trusting the devil. She peeped out the door and saw the horsemen from the night when Orrin landed on her porch. There was no mistaking it. Three of them. Dressed in black with black hats. But wait; she eased back into the room. There were four that night. She'd counted them when they blotted out the stars. Four riding two by two.

The front door opened and the fourth one plowed right into the living room without an invitation. "The horses are ready in the front now. Get the gold and let's get out of here."

"Why the hurry, Santos? No one is around. It is Saturday night. They are all getting ready to go and pray to God tomorrow. We can end this man's suffering with one bullet. Then we can find the woman. She must have gone away for a little while since she isn't in the house now. When she comes home we can play with her like a cat plays with a mouse. Then we will take the gold and go to Mexico with it," Damian said.

Holding her breath so that she didn't give herself away, she bent down and very quietly took the gun from under her bed. It was a .22 rifle. Zeb's best target gun. He and Violet had spent hours in the fields behind their house competing, and more than once she'd beat him soundly when the scores were tallied up. She slipped one bullet in it. One chance was all she had. Someday she'd have a gun that shot bullets as long as she pulled the trigger, but for target practice she only needed one bullet at a time. She exhaled silently. She might be a dead woman right alongside Orrin before the night was done, but there'd be one dead Mexican with a hole between his eyes before she died.

She kicked open the door and threw the gun up on her shoulder all with one smooth motion. "I think you are looking for me," she said.

"Ah, the giant woman," Damian chuckled. "Put that gun down, woman, before you hurt yourself or one of my men."

"Get out of my house, you stinking sorry excuse for a man." She kept her voice steady and calm and looked down her nose at the short man in front of her. If they sensed the

fear that filled her, she and Orrin both would be pushing
up daisies in a few weeks.

"Ah, for that you will pay dearly," Santos said, leering
at her as he took a step in her direction.

"So will you. Don't you take another step toward me.
You are close enough now that I can smell you. I don't
really care which one of you I shoot. It makes me no difference. I just don't want to go to heaven and have to face
the Almighty without being able to say I brought Him a
present to throw to the devil. So whichever one of you that
wants to be my gift, just step right up here, mark the spot,
and I'll make it as painless as possible," she said.

"We only want the gold, lady. Just the gold. Tell us
where it is and I will make these men go away and leave
both of you alone," the oldest of the men said.

"I believe you. Really I do, but I'm not putting this rifle
down until you are out of my house and riding south," she
said.

"You can't shoot that thing anyway," Santos continued
to argue.

"I can shoot the eyes out of a rattlesnake at fifty yards
and not mess up the hide for a nice hatband. And if I'd
been shooting at Orrin Wilde, I wouldn't have just grazed
his shoulders. He'd be as dead as you are about to be." She
lowered the gun slightly until the sights were trained on
Santos's eyes. One little pop and he'd fall backwards into
the piano. She hoped he wouldn't break any of the ornate
fretwork from the edges when he fell.

"We just want the gold," the older man repeated.

"Then go in there and look under his bed. It's under
there. Take it and get out and maybe I won't kill any of
you as you ride away," she said.

Santos ran into the bedroom and drug the heavy saddlebags into the living room. He started to open them but she
clucked her tongue somewhat like a hen calling in the
chickies just before a storm. "No, you're not pouring that

out on my living room floor. If you want it, take it and get out. If there's going to be a blood letting, let's get on with it. Which one of you have decided to die for that gold? I plan on doing my shooting first so one of you step right up and claim this .22 bullet. It's one of those new ones. Hollow point with gilding. Solid lead. Should drop you on the spot before you even know what hits you." She was lying, but since they didn't know what kind of ammunition she had, the thought of a high-powered bullet might put a little fear in their armor.

"Violet," Orrin started. If there was any way to save the gold and both their hides, he fully well intended to try. He hadn't worked eight years, given up the love of his life, and nearly died to watch his fortune walk out the door.

"Let's take it and ride," the older man said.

"Let's kill them and have some fun," Damian said.

"Then you take the bullet she has," Santos said. "I'm with Gramps. It is time for us to go."

Damian's face darkened, and he actually looked like he was about to sprout horns. "You are lucky people today, you are," he finally said. "We are going to ride away. But if you ever come to Mexico you watch your back, because Damian will be there looking for you."

Violet didn't say a word. After all the bravado, she was about to give in to her shaking knees and collapse in front of them. Orrin was as pale as the sheets she'd just put on his bed and if she wasn't mistaken there was blood dripping on her carpet from the right leg of Zeb's pajamas. If she didn't check the wound soon, he might be in big trouble again.

"Good-bye, amigo. If I were you I might keep the giant woman. She holds that gun like she could protect you with it." The one they called Gramps smiled as he walked out the door.

Violet followed them, keeping her gun tight against her shoulder. They might turn on her and Orrin like a pack of feral dogs even yet. She kept Damian in the sights of the rifle until he had the saddlebags loaded and they were riding off at a fast speed. Then she stepped outside and aiming carefully, shot the wide-brimmed black hat from his head. He whipped around in the saddle to frown at her, but she was busy ejecting the shell and reloading. The second zing sent Santos's hat flying in the direction of the coming storm. They rode faster, but not fast enough. She had the casing laying at her feet and a third one in before Orrin could get across the room to see if she was picking them off one at a time. The third bullet pierced the saddle bags they'd stolen from Orrin, but no gold ran out. And the four bandits spurred their horses to a gallop.

"What have you done? There goes all my work for eight years," Orrin said. "And why did you shoot only two hats off?"

"Now those rattlesnakes can fight over who gets to wear the two hats left when the rain is pouring down. I hope it drops hail the size of dinner plates on their sorry bare heads. I have to admit I was aiming at Gramps's hat when I got the saddlebags. Two out of three ain't bad though, is it?" She laid the gun down on the settee and began to laugh. She had a choice: cry, shake, or laugh to get the tension out of her body.

"Violet, are you going to go hysterical on me now? Good grief, I didn't even know you could load a gun." Orrin slumped down in the rocking chair. He wanted to cry like a baby, but the tears wouldn't come.

"Zeb might have had a bald head, Orrin, but he could shoot straight as a sober judge," she dried her eyes and went to lock the front door. Those bandits could still test their luck and return. "You're hurt again. Come on and let's get a fresh bandage and clean you up."

"It's all gone. All eight years worth of hard work. All of it gone," he said in a faraway voice.

"Oh hush, you are alive aren't you?" she snapped.

"Violet, you don't understand," he started.

"Don't you give me that age-old line, Orrin Wilde." She unbuttoned his shirt and took it off like he was a seven year old sleepy boy. "Lean forward," she demanded. She carefully removed the bandage. The entry hole was fine. The blood had come from the nasty exit hole, but it was barely oozing now. She went into the kitchen and returned with a basin of warm water and a bar of soap. He sucked air when the soap hit the raw flesh but she didn't stop until it was clean, doctored with the ointment, and rebandaged. "Now I'm going to bring the tub in the kitchen and fill it with warm water and you can take a real bath. I suppose you're able to lower yourself down in it and if you sit on your knees you should be able to get up without too much trouble," she said.

"Violet, how can you talk about a bath when I've just lost everything I've got. The money is gone. I'm twenty-six years old and I've got nothing. I gave you up for that gold, and now it's all gone," he groaned.

"All goes to show you put too much faith in money. You need a bath, Orrin. There's blood on your back and all the way down your leg. I'll get you a fresh pair of pajamas to put on when you get done. And when are you going to start trusting my judgment? I knew you didn't need to go to California in the beginning. If you'd a waited, we could have had our farm right here in Oklahoma when they had the land run," she argued right back at him.

"Could have. Would have. Maybe. Might. It's all gone," he said.

She wanted to take a bath, not talk about saddlebags full of gold, or gravel either. She was sweating from the fear of those horrid men and she could smell herself. Menfolks bathed first according to Granny Daniels, and Violet wasn't pushing her luck. Not tonight. Not when she'd just held off four vile men. When Orrin got his bath, then she'd dump the water and refill the tub for her own soaking. Maybe that would ease the tension in every muscle in her body.

"Trust me," she said and disappeared into her bedroom. In a few minutes she returned with a sealed envelope and handed it to him.

"What is this?" He looked up so whipped and forlorn she actually felt sorry for him for a few seconds.

"Open it."

Reading a letter right then was the last thing he wanted to do. He didn't care if it was a letter from Violet herself saying that she'd had a change of heart and was madly in love with him. Even if she had a change of heart, he had nothing to offer her. Not now. It had all ridden away with those bandits. He wanted to crawl off in a cave and lick his emotional wounds for a week or two, not read a letter. He looked up at her to find her eyes twinkling and a smile on her face. Well, didn't that just beat all? The only thing that made her smile all week was someone robbing him of his gold. He must have made her even madder than he'd ever imagined by running away and leaving her at the altar, for her to think that it was funny that he was penniless.

"I said open it," she said.

He carefully tore open the envelope and took out a single sheet of paper. It had figures on it and his name at the top, but he had no idea what he was looking at. "What is it?" he asked.

"The night you got shot and landed on my porch, the doctor came from Emma and Jed's after the baby was born to check you. We opened your saddlebags and found all that gold. I sure didn't want it laying around here. Whoever it was that shot you might come back and take it. And they sure enough did just that, didn't they? So I sent it over to Guthrie with the doctor and he put it all in the bank. That is the deposit paper. Your money is safe, Orrin. When you fussed and fumed about the saddlebags I knew you'd not be happy unless you thought they were beside you, so I emptied your other set and filled them up with rocks. I put a few little sacks of sand on the top just in case you ever got the buckle undone," she explained. "Now will you please take your bath so I can get mine."

Chapter Six

Orrin slipped out of his pajamas and eased into the galvanized tub. It had been weeks since he'd had a real, soaking bath. The bandage prevented him from leaning back and really enjoying it to the fullest, but he couldn't complain. He was alive. His money was safe. Suddenly the secure feeling flew out the kitchen window and a fit of furious rage replaced it. He couldn't wash it away with the sweet-smelling soap she'd laid on the chair beside the tub. He couldn't rinse it off with the nice warm water. His nose curled in disgust. His mouth was a hard pressed line, puckering like a dried up raisin. He had been a fool to keep a picture of a loving Violet in his heart all those years. She was just like all women. Interfering. Controlling. He finished his bath, grabbed the towel she'd laid on the chair, and ignored the pain in his shoulders as he wiped the droplets of water from his body.

Violet picked up a dress to work on the hem. She should have finished it days ago. How in the world did Emma find time to sew for the dressmaker and take care of a whole family? Orrin kept Violet so busy she'd scarcely had time to make even two dresses the past week. Not even half of the normal five she had ready on Thursdays. A noise on her porch caused her to throw the collar on the floor. She had the .22 rifle in her hands in one fluid motion. The heel of a boot scraped across the porch and stopped at her door. They were back. Every hair on her neck stood up in prickly fear. She threw the rifle on her shoulder and went to meet the trouble. They weren't about to kick her door in. No, she'd meet them on the porch and this time Damian could go talk to his maker right up close. They could have a brother-to-brother visit and decide which furnace Damian could fire for all eternity.

More scraping told her that they were all four on the porch by now. She eased the bolt back on the thumb lock and threw the door open in a flourish, her finger on the trigger. Sweat beaded up on her upper lip. She hoped she didn't make a mistake and shoot the Gramps fellow. He was as low down as a snake's belly, but it was Damian she intended to take out with her only bullet.

Not one ugly face looked at her from beyond the screen door. So she swung it open and held it there with her foot. There was nothing there but a torrent of rain sprinkled with a few hail stones. She swept the whole porch with the gun, expecting to see them rushing her at any minute. Then something touched the hem of her skirt. She tightened the grip on the gun but lowered her eyes to the porch. A raccoon with a couple of babies scampered across the porch.

She almost giggled at the raccoons, wanting to stay on the dry porch, but at the same time, afraid of the human smell before them. The rain and hail was scary but not as much as the enemy standing in the light of the door. Then there was a noise behind her. The men had come through the kitchen instead of by the front door. She whipped

around, her finger itching to pull the trigger, to find her
sights leveled on Orrin.

"What on earth are you doing?" he asked gruffly.

"Protecting your unthankful, sorry hide," she snapped
right back at him.

"Were they out there again?" he asked.

"No, but I thought they were." She lowered the gun and
kicked the door with her foot, locking it the minute it
slammed shut. "It was just a momma raccoon with her babies hunting a dry place in the storm. I hope those skunks
who were here can't find a dry place. I hope they're sitting
out there in the rain getting wet to the hide."

"I don't trust banks," he said, bluntly.

"What in the world has that got to do with skunks, raccoons, or a storm?" she demanded.

"You could have waited until I was conscious and then
asked me what I wanted to do with my gold. You had no
right to just put it in a bank. I don't trust banks, Violet.
Never have. Daddy trusted in one and we lost everything
when I was little. Remember?" He narrowed his beautiful
brown eyes until they were nothing but slits of dark, flashing rage.

"Well, pardon me!" She waggled her head from side to
side. "You were just bleeding on my rug and about to die.
Besides, you ignorant fool, don't you realize everything
you had would be gone. Those stinking men would have it
now if I hadn't put it in the bank. So stop your moaning
and go to bed. I've had a bad day all because of you, and
I'm going to go take a bath."

"Not until we get this settled," he said, blocking the
kitchen door with his big frame. "It's more than just the
money, Violet. You had no right to do that."

"Then why don't you saddle up that horse out there in
the stable and ride over to the bank in Guthrie. I'm sure
Alford will get right out of bed and go down to the bank
and measure you up the right amount of gold. You can take

it and go to Blue Ridge or to the very devil with it. I don't even care which one you decide on. I'm going through that door and getting my bath ready. If you decide to go, good-bye. That's more than you gave me all those years ago." She laid the gun on the settee and started toward him. Her light gray eyes locked with his brown ones in a battle of wills. He wasn't moving and she wasn't stopping.

When she got so close there was no room left for daggers to fly between them he reached out and wrapped his arms around her. Even if it did hurt, he'd pay the price and be glad to do so. Part of her wanted to snuggle right down in those strong arms but the other part wanted to slap the fire right out of him for touching her when she was so mad. Before she could make up her mind which one to listen to, he'd used the back of his callused hand to tip her chin back and kiss her soundly.

Sparks danced around the room like a million shooting stars. For just a few moments neither of them heard the thunder rolling or saw the lightning flashing through the lace curtains. Violet had forgotten how his kisses affected her. Orrin wanted to pick up the .22 rifle and shoot himself for ever walking away from her.

Finally she broke away and slipped from his embrace. High color crept up her neck and across her cheeks. He moved without saying a word and she went into the kitchen, shutting the door behind her. He slumped down in the rocking chair and wished with all his heart he could go back eight years. If he'd stayed and married her, he still might have convinced her to go to California with him. Now it was entirely too late. She'd kissed him back, prob-ably out of sheer loneliness or perhaps frustration. But the world had not stood still for her like it had for him, because she'd pulled away and shut the door behind her when she went into the kitchen. If she'd seen the shooting stars the way he did, she would have leaned into him for more kisses. No, Orrin had just plain made the biggest mistake of his life when he chose an adventure over a bride. The time had come to pay the fiddler, and Orrin wanted to dance some more. She'd told him to get on Coaly and be gone. But he wasn't that foolish. There was a blinding storm out there and he could scarcely get himself dressed. Picking up a saddle and hoisting himself up on Coaly's back was as impossible as making his heart stop loving Violet Daniels . . . McDonald.

Violet pulled the heavy oval tub out onto the back porch and tilted it, letting the soapy water run out into the yard. Rain blew across her face. It did seem a bit of an extravagance to pour more water into the tub and then have to empty it again when she could grab up a bar of soap and take a natural shower. A grin tickled the corners of her mouth but it didn't materialize. Anna Marie would surely be on her doorstep the next afternoon with a whole list of sins if she got word the widow McDonald was out in the yard in her altogether letting the rain wash her frustrations away.

Her lips still carried the feeling of being kissed when she ran her fingers across them for the tenth time as she hugged the porch post and watched the rain a little longer. She should have gone to California with Orrin, but she couldn't see past the end of the security blanket she'd held onto so tightly. The very thought of leaving Blue Ridge and traveling all the way to the west coast scared the liver out of Violet Daniels. Now, years later, it didn't seem like such a bad idea. But it was too late. Orrin Wilde had grown up and away from Violet. He'd kissed her, yes. Probably more out of pity or gratitude than of anything fervent like they'd shared when they were engaged to be married. If he'd felt the passion stirring in his soul like she had, he would have never dropped his arms and let her go into the kitchen.

She slid down the porch post and sat down with a plop on the wet porch. The rain blew across her face, droplets hanging on her thick eyelashes like morning dew on spring roses. She'd told him to get his horse and go—and he just might try to do it. What would Violet do if he did? Go back to her hum-drum life? Maybe Jim would forgive her for letting a man live in her house and give her another chance. She shuddered. If she had to live the life of an old maid forever, she couldn't encourage Jim Parson's advances. Not now. Not after she'd been spoiled by that one burning kiss. It might have to be enough to carry her until her dying day, and if it was, then so be it. She wasn't settling for anything less than that. Yet, she couldn't trust Orrin. Not after the way he'd so spitefully ran away. She couldn't trust him and she didn't want anyone else. Simple as it sounded, that was the way it was.

She was soaked to the skin when she finally went back into the kitchen, dragging the tub behind her. She set it in the middle of the kitchen floor and began to fill it with warm water from the reservoir on the side of the stove. Then she remembered she hadn't laid out a thing for her bath. Her clean clothing was in her bedroom, and she looked like a drowned kitten. Kitten nothing. More like a drowned full grown mountain lion. Violet was too big and tall to ever come across as a kitten in anyone's eyes.

Orrin was still sitting in the rocking chair when she slid through the kitchen door, dripping water all the way across the living room floor. He didn't turn around. He didn't have to see her to know what she looked like. He'd carried that vision with him for so long, he knew every feature in her beautiful face, every nuance in her graceful walk. "So, you finished so soon with your bath?" he asked, talking around the lump in his throat.

"Haven't started it yet," she said. "Had to dump the water from the tub and refill it." The reflection in the mirror on the back of her door almost made her weep. Hair straggling down from her neat bun, hanging in limp strands down her back, over her left shoulder, and even in her eyes. Her blouse had blood smudges on it from where she'd taken care of Orrin's wounds after the men rode off. She surely didn't feel like some rifle-toting mean woman right then. Her pride lay at her feet in a puddle of rainwater dripped through a day's worth of cleaning and cooking in her light blue dress. Well, there wasn't one thing to do but pick up her clean things, her special gardenia soap, and a towel and go back to the kitchen. With any luck at all, he'd be in his room and wouldn't see the big horse of a woman that Anna Marie talked about.

When the bedroom door opened, he looked up. His face reddened when he noticed that her dress was soaked. She'd dumped his bath water out into the driving rain and gotten wet in doing so. Humiliation filled his masculine soul. Even wet, she was the most beautiful woman he'd ever laid eyes upon. He wanted so badly to push that errant strand of dark hair back behind her ear. But to touch her again would be courting disaster. She would surely toss him out on his ear, and his pride couldn't take another whipping that evening. She'd saved his life. Drawn his bath. Emptied it. Fought with him and won. His dignity lay in a battered heap at his bare feet.

Well, so much for hoping he didn't see her in her state of disgusting disarray. She held her dry night rail and robe away from her dripping body, and holding her back straight and erect, went back to the kitchen without saying a word. She laid the pile of clothes on the table and sat down on the floor. No matter how much front she'd just put on, she felt like weeping. Sobbing until all the tears inside her heart were gone. Who was it that said, "Tears on the outside fall to the ground and are slowly washed away. Tears on the inside fall on the soul. And stay and stay and stay." Some poet she'd read during those long, lonely evenings she spent alone while Zeb was out on the train. Whoever it was must have known Orrin Wilde sometime in their lifetime.

Chapter Seven

She chose a dark blue dress from her closet that Sunday morning. It had a fitted waist and a flounce ruffle at the end of the skirt. The collar laid back with a fine edge of lace, with matching lace-covered buttons all the way down the front. It was one of her favorite dresses, one she usually saved for weddings and important occasions, but if they were going to crucify her that morning, she might as well be dressed well. She set her hat at just the right angle and slipped in a long hat pin to secure it. Then she picked up her shawl and with a whirl let it fall over her shoulders. She looked at the end result in the mirror. Maybe she should have chosen something in scarlet so when Anna Marie pinned a sign on her back branding her for a harlot, her dress would match. That brought a smile to her face even if it didn't quite reach her light gray eyes.

When she opened the bedroom door Orrin was sitting in the rocking chair. He was fully dressed in his best dark trousers, a white shirt buttoned all the way to the top, and

63

his boots, though worn, had been brushed. He had a single drop of blood on his chin where he'd cut himself shaving, but other than that he was so handsome Violet practically gasped. Between the vision of him sitting there looking like some dark prince from an English novel, and the realization that he was ready to leave, her knees turned to quaking mush.

"Well, don't you look lovely this morning, Violet," he said.

"Thank you, Orrin. You don't look so shabby yourself." She tried to drink in every single feature. That one last memory would have to keep her all the way to the grave. From the way his hair was combed straight back to the single little drop of dried blood on his face. She'd never forget any of it.

"You'll have to drive since I can't do that yet, and I don't think I can help you down from the buggy, but I expect I won't embarrass you too much," he said, ducking his head to keep from looking up into those mesmerizing gray eyes.

"What are you talking about?" she asked.

"Church," he said. "It's Sunday mornin' and I expect we're going to church. You're all dolled up and we always did go to church on Sunday down in Blue Ridge. That is where we're going this morning, isn't it?"

"Of course it is," she said nervously. "Only I usually walk to church. It's only a couple of blocks. I could hitch up the horses if you think it's too far?"

"No, I can make it. We could leave early and go slow," he said, grinning. He'd walk a mile over hot coals and not mind a bit of it, just to be able to sit beside her in church.

"We'd better get started then. You sure you're up to this?" she asked. He'd actually looked pale earlier that morning at the breakfast table and had barely picked at his eggs. She'd wondered if infection could have set up from the bandits making his back bleed again.

"If you'll pretend you are holding my arm, it would make it easier. Then if I start to fall, you could brace me up," he said, crooking his left arm when they were on the porch.

She slipped her arm through the loop and was only mildly surprised when her bare fingertips brushed his. The shock glued her feet to the porch for a few seconds, but she didn't gasp or sigh. Orrin Wilde would never know the second time around what an effect he or his kisses had on her.

"Now, tell me about these stores as we pass them," he said, keeping his pace very slow. Church didn't matter nearly as much as the time they would spend walking there and back. "There's the general store, I guess?"

"Yes, it's grown a lot in the past year. Used to be we just bought a few things there and then went into Guthrie for a major purchase about three times a year. But Dodsworth is growing and Duncan, the owner of the store, is keeping more," she said, amazed that her voice wasn't coming out high and squeaky.

By the time they got to the church yard he'd asked a million questions about every house or business they passed. Wagons and buggies were everywhere. Violet recognized the Thomas wagon and wondered if Emma had come to church that morning. The baby would only be a week old, but farm women weren't pampered like city women often were. A pang of guilt hit her in the soft part of her heart because she hadn't been out to see Emma and the new baby. Not once had she taken dinner to the family or offered to take Molly in and take care of her. Fine friend she'd been all week while she was nursing Orrin back to health, fighting every step of the way with him over every little thing. It was nothing short of a miracle that they didn't find something to argue about on the way to the church. Rest assured, she reminded herself, the day is still young and we will have at least one argument before bedtime.

Suddenly, she missed the peace and quiet she shared with Zeb. Then that sassy little voice in the back of her mind reminded her that monotonous rut was just what she'd hated last Sunday at this time.

"Oh, hush," she whispered.

"I didn't say a word," Orrin said. Mercy, she'd been about half nice on the way to the church and now she was right back to her old sassy, spiteful self. Maybe she was ashamed of him now that they were ready to walk into the church house proper?

"I wasn't talking to you, Orrin Wilde. And don't you be asking me any questions either about who I was talking to. I hope you like kids because I'm planning on insisting that Emma and Jed come home with us for dinner. I haven't even been out there to hold the new baby or see her either," she snapped.

"I love kids," he said. "How many kids are we talking about?"

"Five." She swept her skirts to one side so they could go through the double doors together.

"But I thought they'd only been married a little over a year?" he whispered.

"I'll explain it all later. Looks like we're late enough we get the front pew," she said with a sigh.

"Guess it won't hurt us to sit up there," he said, grinning.

"Speak for yourself," she said under her breath and proceeded to walk up the church aisle. Every face in the church turned to see Violet's man, as they'd come to call him over the backyard fences and from the back side of hands when they gossiped. She caught Emma's eye and smiled when she saw the pink bundle in her arms. Jed still looked like his feet were barely hitting the ground. The other four kids—Sarah, Mary, Jimmy, and Molly—were lined up on the same pew with them just like every Sunday morning. Anna Marie frowned spitefully when Violet and Orrin passed her pew. She held eight month old Al in her arms and he squirmed and fussed loudly. Maggie Listen winked at her, and it was that wink that almost put Violet over the edge into hysterical laughter. Here she was twenty-six years old, a widow, and independent as a one-eyed mule. She had a man literally living under the same roof with her, and she expected the whole world to come crashing down around her shoulders that morning at church.

"We would like to welcome Violet McDonald's boarder to our services this morning. I understand they've known each other since they were children and fate brought him to her door a week ago after some violent, evil men tried to kill him. We must never underestimate the power of God. He knew that Orrin Wilde was in need of help and sent him right to a friendly woman's door." Preacher Elgin smiled down upon them. "Also we are welcoming the newest edition to our community, Miss Lalie Joy Thomas. She was born last Sunday night after services. Now I'd say Emma Thomas is a true Christian woman. Waits until after church services on Sunday night to have her baby and then is back with us the next Sunday. Hasn't missed a thing the good Lord has to say to her. We are sorry to report that Duncan is under the weather this morning and can't join us. We'll miss his voice when we sing. And my son-in-law, Alford, was unable to come to services this morning. He's under the weather also. Now if you'll open your books to number one sixty-two we'll start off this morning with a song to lift our voices to the Lord for his blessings this week."

Violet found the page and shared her book with Orrin. That alone would cause a stir amongst the women in the church. A woman, widow or otherwise, didn't share a hymnal with a man if they weren't serious about each other. It was as sacred a tradition as sharing a picnic with one on the creek banks. Jim Parsons probably had his nails and hammer all ready to tack her wanton hide to the cross right after the final prayer.

She'd forgotten what a fine singing voice Orrin had until he harmonized with her, bringing a beautiful smile down from Preacher Elgin in the pulpit. After the song, the preacher opened his Bible and began to preach on the commandment about loving thy neighbor as thyself. Violet didn't know if the text was chosen to make her feel better about taking care of Orrin in spite of the wagging tongues or if it was picked to highlight her faults for not helping Emma more the past week. Either way, she had trouble keeping her mind on the sermon when her shoulder was touching Orrin's.

After the final prayer, Jim Parsons just nodded in her direction and disappeared out the back door. Violet almost sighed in relief. She expected him to have something haughty if passive to say to her. Anna Marie's eyes started at her toes and traveled all the way to the hat on her head. She shook her head in unbelief and said, "Remember what I told you. He's never going to be interested. Oh, I've got to go. Little Al has started to walking. Early for a baby to walk at only eight months, but then he is very smart."

"Must take after his father," Violet said.

"Of course he does." Anna Marie laughed. "Gets his smart brain from Alford and his beauty from me."

"Oh, Emma." Violet ignored Anna Marie and turned quickly to hug her friend. Emma passed the pink bundle to her outstretched arms and Violet's heart was lost the first time she laid eyes on the sweet baby girl in the blankets. Lalie Joy had a head full of Jed's dark hair, Emma's gorgeous eyes and mouth, and Molly's little ears. She opened her eyes widely and stared at Violet, the two of them forming a bonding friendship right then and there. It wasn't until she clasped the baby to her breast that Violet began to ache for a baby of her own. Not once in the whole time she was married to Zeb did she ever let herself want a child. She'd known when she married him that children weren't even an option. Zeb had had a bad spell with mumps in his youth and couldn't father children.

And now, now that she'd accepted the fact she would be an old widow woman, it was cruel for her body to want a baby. Emma would just have to share Lalie Joy with her. That's all there was to it.

"Pretty baby." Orrin looked over her shoulder at the tiny little human all dressed in pink. "Girl, I would suppose?"

"Yep," Molly said. "It's a girl. My Emma had it for me to play with since the other kids get to go to school. I wanted a girl baby so me and Emma could make pretty clothes for it. Her name is Lalie Joy and my name is Molly. Are you the man who's sleeping with Violet?"

"Well, I'm staying at Violet's house," Orrin stammered. "I'm right glad to meet you, Miss Molly. And I think your new sister is almost as pretty as you. I don't think she's going to have your blonde hair, though."

"Nope. She's going to have black hair and blue eyes. I think I like you. What's your name?"

"I'm Orrin Wilde," he said seriously.

"Daddy Jed, come here and meet my Orrin. He's the man who sleeps with Violet," Molly said at the top of her lungs as she ran through the people to the door, where Jed was talking with the preacher about Lalie Joy's christening date.

"Oh, my," Violet said, blushing.

"Orrin Wilde, I'm Emma Thomas." Emma offered her hand. "Don't worry about Molly. She says what she thinks. I'm afraid I encourage that. She was such a shy little thing when Jed and I married last year."

"I'm glad to meet you, Emma. Violet has talked about you so much I feel like we've already met." He shook her hand gingerly.

"Hello, Orrin." Jed held out his hand. "You must have impressed our Molly. She referred to Emma as *my Emma* from the first time she laid eyes on her. Now she has a *my Orrin*. You better be careful, though. She's pretty possessive."

"Whew, she does speak her mind, doesn't she?" Orrin blushed again.

"Yes, she does." Jed grinned. "You're doing pretty good for the condition I saw you in last week. Didn't know if you'd live or not the way you was bleeding on Violet's floor last Sunday night."

"Was only because of her care that I've lived, I'm sure," Orrin said.

"We'll continue this conversation at the house," Violet announced without handing the baby back to Emma. Just one more minute to savor the sweet smell of the baby and the way just holding her made Violet's heart fairly well float out of her chest. "I insist that you all come to my house for dinner. You and Jimmy can twist off a couple of chicken's heads and pluck them. I'll fry them up for dinner."

"Can't turn that down," Jed said. "Besides, Emma has been cooped up for a week, and she's leaning toward starting a fight with me. So maybe a few hours in your presence will keep her out of trouble."

"Or you out off the cot out in the tack room for the night," Emma smarted off to him.

"Wouldn't bet on Violet keeping her out of trouble," Orrin said.

"That's enough out of you. There's not even a cot in my tack room so you'll have a pile of hay and a saddle for a pillow." Violet handed the baby back to Emma grudgingly and pointed at Orrin. "Now let's go. These children are probably starving to death."

"I am, Violet. I am starving to death. I might even die on the way to your house," Molly chattered. "Can I walk with you and my Orrin? My Emma, can I walk with them? My Orrin needs me to hold his hand. Jimmy said some mean men shot him in the back, and I think if he holds my hand he'll feel all better."

"Of course you can," Emma said with a smile. "But don't hold his hand too tight. It might make his back hurt. We'll be there soon as we can run the other three kids down," she said to Violet.

Orrin propped his hip against the corner of the house and watched Jimmy and Jed chase down three young fryers. Jimmy wanted to get the chopping ax down but Jed said it wasn't necessary. They'd just twist their heads off with a flick of the wrist. Violet already had a pot of water to the boiling stage and setting on the back porch. Jed used a sharp knife to remove the feet and entrails; then he dipped the birds into the hot water. He and Jimmy both worked at plucking them.

"Who's kids are these?" Orrin finally asked. "Yours or Emma's? Neither one of you look old enough to have kids this age."

"They're ours now. My sister, Joy, and her husband came to Oklahoma with me from up north for the land run. We got joining sections of land. Things were going great guns until they both come down with cholera that year and died. I inherited their land and four kids. There's Sarah, Mary, Jimmy, and Molly. And now we've got one of our own, Lalie Joy," Jed explained as he pulled feathers from the white chickens.

"I see," Orrin said.

"So what's this I hear about you and Violet knowing each other down in Texas? Doc said you two grew up together," Jed said.

"We did. She was the prettiest girl in the whole county. When we was fourteen I finally got as tall as her and felt like I could ask her to be my girl." Orrin chuckled.

"Oh, then you were more than just acquaintances?" Jed raised an eyebrow.

"We were engaged at one time. I made a big mistake and it's too late to go back now. I'll get well in another week or so and then I'll go on home to Blue Ridge. I'm going to buy a farm and build me a house. Find me a couple of good dogs," Orrin said.

Jed heard the hurt in his voice. He'd been in Orrin's shoes about a year ago, but things had worked out for him and Emma. Didn't look like it would for Orrin and Violet, by the tone of Orrin's voice. They might have a past, but didn't seem like there would be a future. Too bad. Jed's first impression was to like the man.

"We got a whole litter of new puppies," Jimmy said. "Ginger, our momma dog and Buster, the poppa dog, have got ten babies. Want one of them?"

"Well, now, I don't know," Orrin started.

"Good dogs. Chase coons all night," Jed said. "Jimmy can pick out one for you and bring it in tonight when we come to church. Got a gold-looking one that you might like. Give you something to do while you're recuperating."

"In that case, I'd love one," Orrin said. "Jimmy, you reckon you could pick them feathers a little faster? My stomach is getting pretty hungry."

"I reckon so," Jimmy said, smiling. "Tell the truth, mine is too. And fried chicken is my favorite Sunday dinner."

In the house, Sarah rocked Lalie Joy in Violet's sewing rocker while Violet bustled about the kitchen. She'd made Emma sit at the table, forbidding her to even peel a potato. "It's bad enough I didn't get out there to help you this week. So this is one meal you aren't helping with. That or the dishes either. When it's done, me and these two girls are doing clean up. Right, Mary?"

Mary rolled her eyes toward the ceiling. "Of course, I'll be glad to help wash dishes, Violet. But only if you'll tell me all about that handsome man you've got living with you. I've just got to tell all the girls in the church yard tonight that I got to sit right up to the table with him. If you don't want him, will you please hold him down until I grow up?"

Violet's face turned redder than the pickled beets she emptied into a fancy bowl. "Honey, you don't want that man. He might be handsome but he's a heartbreaker."

"How do you know?" Mary challenged.

"Just take it from a woman who does know," Violet said. "Now you run out to the spring house and get a gallon of milk. Did I tell you I made that triple layer chocolate cake with pecans that you like so well? Stirred it up yesterday before the bandits came. I was fearful that they'd come to steal my cake and you'd be disappointed."

That brought on a multitude of questions about the near escape she'd had with the four would-be robbers. Mary couldn't be budged from her place by the door until she'd heard every last word of the story. If she couldn't hold court with the other little girls in the church yard about the handsome Mr. Wilde then she could at least report the story of Violet protecting him by staving off a bunch of evil, half-monster men with her rifle.

Once Mary had skipped off to the spring house, Emma raised an eyebrow at Violet. "Oh, okay," Violet said, and sighed. Sarah kept rocking the baby, but neither Emma nor Violet had a worry about saying anything in front of that girl. She was as closed-mouthed as her sister was loquacious. Mary could be seen in the school yard in the center of a bunch of little girls every day telling stories. Sarah was her opposite.

"So what's the story with you and Orrin?" Emma asked. "And you better speak fast or else Mary will be back."

"We grew up together, fell in love, and were engaged. I was standing at the altar when the preacher said Orrin wasn't there. He'd run away to California to work an old gold mine his uncle left him when he died. End of story. I cried and married Zeb. Orrin ended up on my door step. I've took care of him. He'll be gone in a few days. Real end of story." Violet drained the liquid from a jar of carrots, shook them out in a pan, added a quarter pound of sweet cream butter and half a cup of honey, and set them on the back burner of the stove.

"Wow, did he really leave you at the altar?" Sarah's eyes bugged out. "That was awful. I would have cried too. Do you still love him?"

Emma looked up just in time to see the pain in her friend's face. The answer was written there as clearly as if it had been put there with indelible ink right on her forehead. Violet McDonald still did love that long, tall drink of cold Texas water out there in the yard.

"That's a hard question to answer, Sarah. I'll have to think on it a while," Violet said about the time Mary came toting in a gallon jar of milk. "We'll skim the thick cream off the top for the mashed potatoes. Here's a bowl, Miss Mary. You can do that for me."

"Did you really shoot their hats off?" Mary asked.

"Yes, I did," Violet said.

"Will you teach me how to shoot?"

"Of course I will. If Emma doesn't mind. When you get sixteen, you come around here and I'll take you down to the creek and we'll shoot target."

"I don't mind one bit," Emma said. "Girls should be able to take care of themselves. If you hadn't known how, I wouldn't be sitting at your table right now watching you work your fingers to the bone making my family a meal."

"Momma, I think Lalie Joy is ready to eat," Sarah said. "You come sit in the rocker. It's more comfortable. I'll help Violet. Can I make the biscuits? Momma taught me how this summer. She says I've got a good hand at it."

"Of course you can," Violet said.

"But don't you be bragging to Orrin about it," Mary said, tilting her chin up defiantly. "I'm still not sure if I want to wait on him, but he's mine if I do."

"Who is whose?" Jed asked, bringing in the bowl full of cut-up chicken ready to roll in buttermilk and flour and fry.

"Nothing." Mary sniffed dramatically. "We was talking

about girl things. You boys don't tell us what you talk about so we don't have to tell neither."

Orrin caught Violet's eye and winked. High color filled her cheeks. Mercy, she hadn't blushed in years and years and this man had her red half the day already. "You better get on in there and find a place to sit down," she ordered Orrin with a point of her finger. "You been up so long, you'll be falling in a heap if you don't rest."

"I'm not tired," he challenged. To obey her when it was just the two of them was one thing. To be ordered around in front of another man didn't set too well with him.

"I didn't ask if you was tired," she said. "I said for you to sit down. I've got dinner to cook, Orrin Wilde. I don't have time to stop and take care of you."

"Okay, you two, stop your arguing." Molly stomped her foot. "If you don't, you'll go to the bedroom like Momma and Daddy Jed and then we'll all have to wait for dinner. And I'm hungry now."

Jed and Emma both blushed and began to laugh. Sarah blushed and hid her face behind her hands. Jimmy darted out the back door, and Mary rolled her eyes again. Violet looked at Orrin, who was grinning like a possum eating grapes through a barbed wire fence. She held her hands to keep from reaching across the table and slapping the smile right off his handsome face.

"Molly, darling," Violet finally said, "take your Orrin to the front porch and keep him and your Daddy Jed there until I call them to dinner. Men folks don't belong in the kitchen."

"Yes, ma'am." Molly grabbed each of them by a hand. "You two come with me. Neither one of you know how to behave. I'm going to take you to the porch swing for a visit before we all have to go hungry."

Chapter Eight

Orrin crossed his arms over his chest and watched Violet from the corner of his eye. She drove the buggy with easy competence and grace. But then she'd said that she had driven into Guthrie every Tuesday to get Zeb and then on Thursday morning to take him back. So she'd had lots of experience.

Violet didn't need to look at Orrin to know that he was looking at her. Her skin came close to igniting in flames every time she felt his eyes on her. More than likely he was giving thanks that he wouldn't have to endure her presence much longer. A couple of weeks at the most, since he was healing so nicely. He'd even helped get the horses hooked up to the buggy this morning. He'd been quite taken with Jed and Jimmy and especially Molly yesterday, so when she told him she was getting up before dawn to go out to their place and do Emma's laundry this week, he'd jumped right on the idea.

The farmhouse lay just below a small rise created by the

rolling hills. The old house was still there. The little one bedroom, lofted cabin Jed and his brother-in-law had built. Just north of it stood the new house. Jed had been worried that the builders wouldn't have it done by the time the new baby arrived. But they'd worked long hours and the Thomas family had moved into it a month before. It was a two story, pristine white with a wide verandah wrapping around all four sides. After Jed finally swallowed his pride and let Emma's father give them the house for a wedding gift, he got right into the design and building of the place. It had to face the east so Emma could watch the sun come up from her kitchen window, and it had to have a porch swing on the back porch and a widow's walk above the porches so Emma could look at the moon and stars.

"Quite a place," Orrin commented.

"Yes, it is. A wedding gift from Emma's father. They started out in that little one right there and lived there until a couple of months ago," she pointed toward the small cabin. "They keep saying they'll tear it down. I'll believe it when I see it. There's too many memories in that little cottage. It's where they fought their way into a solid marriage."

"Oh, you mean you have to fight your way into marriage? I thought two people fell in love and got married," he said while she parked the buggy at the edge of the barn.

"That's what happens when you think," she said with a frown. "You always get it wrong when you've got ten minutes to think about it. Jed was like that, too. Thank goodness he came to his senses. You need help getting out of the buggy?"

"No thank you, ma'am," he said, frost hanging from his words. Women! God surely had a sense of humor when he made them to provoke a man to anger. A man couldn't live with them and it was sure enough against the law to shoot them.

"Well, then do it yourself, Mr. Do-It-Yourself," she

smarted right back at him. Mercy Heavens, she'd never talked to Zeb one day like that. Never had they snapped at each other. But then, never had he kissed her like Orrin had done on Saturday night either. How did Emma and Jed live in such a topsy-turvy world?

"Hey, Orrin," Jimmy called, running out the back door. "Come on out to the dog pens and look at the puppy I got picked out for you. I heard Violet and Momma saying ya'll were coming here today so I didn't bring him to church last night. You can take him home with you today."

"No you aren't," Violet said. "I won't have a puppy making messes on my rug. You aren't taking a dog to my house."

"I just might, madam," Orrin informed her. Be danged if that sassy woman was going to control every blessed thing he did or thought. He'd take a dog home if he wanted to. Maybe he'd even take two dogs. A male and a female so that he could start his own crop of coon dogs.

"Orrin Wilde!" She stared him right in the eyes without blinking.

"Violet Daniels?" He met her challenge.

"My Orrin!" Molly jumped off the porch and ran as fast as her chubby little legs could carry her to his side. "Come in my house and see my new bedroom. We gots lots of bedrooms up the stairs. Momma and Daddy Jed has got a bedroom and a little one off to the side for baby Lalie in the downstairs, but us kids has all got a room up the stairs. Come on. Why are you looking at Violet so mean? You two ain't fightin' again, are you?"

"No, pretty little lady, we aren't fighting again," Orrin said, laughing.

"No dogs," Violet said.

"One or two?" Orrin asked so quietly she was the only one who heard.

If looks could kill, he would have dropped right there in the Oklahoma red dust with Molly tugging at his pants legs and Jimmy yelling at him from the dog pens back behind the house. He smiled at Violet and told Molly he'd have to see her room up the stairs a little later. He'd promised Jimmy that he'd go look at puppies. At that, Molly declared she'd just go with him.

Violet found Mary and Sarah already dipping warm water into the wash tubs. She rolled up her sleeves and grabbed up the white sheets to begin the laundry. She set the rub board into the water and took out all her frustrations on the sheets. When she had them thoroughly washed she wrung them out and handed them to Sarah, who began to job of dousing them up and down in the rinsing tub.

"Well, there you are and already elbow deep," Emma said, coming in from the bedroom. "Miss Lalie Joy just finished her breakfast. I could do the rinsing."

"No, next week is soon enough for you to be lifting heavy clothes. I might come on and help that week, too. After that it might not hurt you to pick up things. But six weeks need to go by before you lift the tubs. Now that's an order." Violet tried to keep her voice light and happy. It didn't come out that way.

"Fighting again, huh?" Emma chuckled.

"Just on an hourly basis," Violet said. "He wants dogs now. Maybe even two of them. Zeb never allowed animals in the house."

"Zeb is dead. What do you allow?" Emma asked honestly. She sat down in the rocking chair and picked up a dress she'd finished making for Sarah the week before. All it needed was button holes, buttons, and the hem. She'd work on it while Violet and the girls put out the washing. If Violet and Orrin didn't wake up pretty soon and see that their hearts were doing a courtship dance, then Emma decided she'd intervene. But she'd give them a couple of weeks. Thank goodness Aunt Beulah had meddled in her and Jed's business last year or there wouldn't be a Lalie Joy sleeping peacefully in her cradle in the bedroom.

"Did I tell you I got a telegram last week from Daddy and Eulalie? She had her baby a couple of weeks early. Scared Daddy at first. It's been a long time since I was born so he's gotten rusty," Emma said.

"Boy or girl?" Violet's voice softened.

"Two boys. Not so big since there was two of them, but Daddy said in the telegram they are both healthy and Eulalie is happy and doing great. They named them Stuart after my grandfather Cummins and Montgomery after her father. So I've got a daughter and two little brothers all within a few days of each other. Strange world, isn't it Violet?"

"You don't know how strange." Violet began rubbing the kitchen towels she'd tossed into the wash tub.

"I think I do." Emma smiled brightly. "Remember where I was a year ago today? Getting married to a man I'd just met in a general store."

"Guess so." Violet rubbed the towels violently.

"Momma, Momma!" Molly hit the back door in a run, letting it slam behind her. "My Orrin picked out a puppy. It's a girl dog and he says he's going to name it Molly after me. Ain't that good. It's the one with the black ears. I just know my Orrin is going to love his Molly."

"I'm sure he is," Emma said, gathering Molly to her side and kissing her blonde pigtails. "I sure do love my Molly."

"Sure you do. You're supposed to love your kids." Molly wiggled out of her embrace and ran back outside, shouting something about going to talk to her Orrin some more.

Violet set her jaw in anger. "I told him no."

Mary's ears picked up the tone and she smiled. A story. Violet and Orrin were fighting over a dog. Oh, if only Sunday wasn't a whole week away and school hadn't just let out last week. Six days before she could tell all about it after church. But by then there might be more to the story.

"Buster still comes in when it storms. Since that tornado he's scared to death of the thunder." Emma laughed. "Jed said dogs didn't belong in the house. What does it hurt? We had a big old fight about it when Buster got hurt that time. Last week when it thundered and he whined at the door, Jed was the one who let him inside."

"My daddy didn't like dogs in the house either," Violet said.

"What do you like?" Emma asked again. "If you don't like animals then put the puppy in the stable. Lock the door and she'll whine and carry on but you won't hear it. Believe me, the horses won't care. But if it's just a pride thing because you want to win the argument, it isn't worth it."

Violet looked up to see Emma studying her. She was wearing her feelings on her sleeve and Emma, being her best friend, could see what was really bothering her. "There, I think those sheets are rinsed a plenty. Let's wring them out. Think you two girls are big enough to get them on the line?"

"Sure we are," Sarah said. "We got Buster tied so he won't chase in around them. Come on, Mary. Let's go get them on the line."

"I'll let these clothes soak for a little while." Violet smiled at Emma. "If you can't lick 'em, join 'em. I'm going out to see the new puppies for a few minutes."

"I do believe you are getting the hang of this thing," Emma said.

"Don't you dare put your hands in this water. Just sit there and hem that dress." Violet shook her finger at Emma.

"I'll do it," Emma said.

Orrin was sitting on the ground in front of the momma dog. He had a big grin on his face and a puppy in his lap, letting it lick him right in the face. Jimmy and Jed sat beside him, letting puppies crawl all over them, too. It must be a male thing, she thought as she crossed her arms over her chest. What on earth could be so amusing about a bunch of silly dogs?

"Want to thank you for helping out today," Jed said

when he finally noticed that she was there. "Me and Jimmy could have helped the girls, but we'd a been all day doing what you can get done in a couple of hours. Women folks are just more organized in the house than us men. We got all thumbs when it comes to house work."

"You're welcome," she said. "You giving those things away?"

"Yep, Orrin picked out a female so he can start his own line when he gets down to Blue Ridge," Jimmy said.

She took a deep breath and plopped right down on the green grass beside the momma dog. In a matter of minutes, two puppies realized there was a lap they hadn't explored and were jumping around, trying to lick her cheeks and nibble her fingers at the same time. Violet was amazed at how soft and cuddly they were. She picked one up and buried her face in the dark brown fur on its back. It wiggled and squirmed but it didn't leave her lap.

Orrin could scarcely believe his eyes. She'd said he couldn't have a puppy, and yet there she sat, her eyes sparkling in amusement at them frolicking all over and around her. Women! He'd never understand a one of them. Not if he lived to be a hundred years old. "This one is mine," he said, taunting her.

"So this one here is mine." She held up the brown dog. "They can sleep in the stables together. That way they won't whine so much. They'll have each other for company. By the time you go to Blue Ridge my dog will be used to my place and won't even miss your dog."

Orrin shook his head. Surely his ears had misunderstood what he just heard. Violet was taking a dog home, too. But he didn't miss the tone when she said "my" house and "my" dog. It would never be our house or our dogs. Not with Violet. He'd made a mistake that couldn't ever be rectified. "What if they want to come inside?" he asked.

"Oh, she'll probably have them eating at the kitchen table and shedding hair on the settee," Jed said. "I've been taught my whole life that dogs didn't come in the house. Emma changed that. Buster whines at the door if he smells a storm cloud coming up from south Texas and she's got him around the neck talking baby talk to him."

"Violet?" Orrin baited her. One part of his heart chastised him for doing it; the other part wanted him to keep it up until he finally won one of the battles. Just one fight before he left in a few days so he wouldn't drag his dignity behind him and Molly when he went to Texas.

"Just don't give my dog to anyone else today," she said, ignoring Orrin altogether. "Think he'll have to be tied on wash day?"

"Betcha he will. Only, your dog is a she-dog, not a he-dog. But she might take after Buster, since that's her papa." Jimmy laughed and pointed at Buster, lying in the yard and looking sheepish about his fate. "Buster never has learned to leave them sheets alone. Emma tries to beat him to death with the broom when he gets loose, but she loves him, too. What're you going to name this dog?" Jimmy asked.

"I'll have to think about it. I've never named anything in my life, so I can't do it on a whim. I'll have to think long and hard about it. Now I'm going back in and finish up the laundry then we'll get some lunch on the table before we go back to the house and do our Monday chores." She kissed the puppy right on her nose and set her down. Orrin wished with all his heart right then that he could trade places with that brown pup.

She marched back into the house with a lighter heart than she'd had in weeks. She'd shocked the socks off that man of hers. *Hers?* She stopped dead in her tracks for a few moments, trying to sort that thought out before she went back into the house. Mercy, but she didn't intend to ever think about him like that, since it was pretty plain he didn't want anything to do with her. Butting up against everything she said or did all the time. That wasn't the way of two people who cared about each other.

"Well, did you let him have a puppy?" Emma asked when Violet opened the back door. "They are pretty cute critters aren't they?"

"Yes, they are. I picked out one for me while I was out there. If he's taking a dog home, then I'll take one, too. I bet I picked out the best one," Violet said mischievously. "And when he leaves his dog is going to cry for mine. But mine is going to love me so much, it won't ever cry for him or his dog."

I'd be willing to bet those dogs never are separated. At least not for very long, Emma thought, as she expertly slip-stitched the hem in place.

Orrin sat on a barrel and watched Jed work on his equipment all morning. They talked about farming and what a man would have time to get planted if he got a late start. "Guess next spring would really be the time to get a jump on crops. A man buying land this late in the year would do well to use his time to build his home this summer and fall, huh?"

"That's the way I'd do it," Jed said. "You got your heart set on Blue Ridge?"

"I did have. It's all I've thought about for eight years. And I've got the money to buy a good chunk of land, some cattle, and put up a house. But you know, I really do like this part of the world. Know any land around here for sale?"

"Know a prime piece about a quarter of a mile on down that dirt road out there." Jed pointed to the south. "Only problem I see is that it's owned by Violet, and I don't expect you'd want to buy it."

"Ain't that I wouldn't buy it," Orrin said. "She wouldn't sell it to me. Says she can't wait until I can put a saddle on Coaly and get gone. I'd leave tomorrow just to get out of her hair. I know I'm a thorn in her side. But I can't get that saddle on or off and Blue Ridge is a long ride from here for a man in my shape," Orrin confided quietly.

"I see," Jed said, reading volumes between the lines. He'd been where Orrin was. He'd walked a mile in his shoes just a year ago. "I reckon I could help you with that problem if you've a mind to stay here. I reckon I could buy that land from Violet and then turn around and sell it to you. You could maybe get the same men who put this house up to get you one built by wintertime."

"I can't stay with Violet until wintertime, and there isn't a hotel in Dodsworth," Orrin lamented.

"Well, I guess you could stay out there in our old house. It's big enough for one man to rattle around in. We had four kids and me and Emma out there for more'n a year," Jed said.

"Violet Daniels would shoot you graveyard dead, man." Orrin chuckled. "You're her friend, and Emma is her best friend. I wouldn't come between ya'll for the whole world, let alone a piece of land."

"You think on it, Orrin. You change your mind, come around and we'll talk again," Jed said. He would bet his new hat that Orrin Wilde would be on his door step in a couple of weeks with his hat in his hand. Orrin didn't realize that he wouldn't be coming between them for long. He'd be joining them.

"Thank you, Jed. Thank you a lot. Now hand me some of that tack. I can at least rub a little saddle soap in it and do that job for you while I'm setting here," Orrin said.

"Might hurt your back," Jed said.

"Probably will, but if I don't exercise this thing, it'll get even stiffer," he said.

The sun was straight up in the sky when Jed said he was going inside to check on the womenfolks. Jimmy said he had to go check on the puppies one more time before Violet and Orrin took two of them away from their momma. He figured they needed to nurse one more time so they'd be good and full when they got to their new home. Orrin kept softening the bridle he was working on until he finished.

Just as he stood up, Violet stepped into the barn. She was a picture, with the sleeves of her light blue and white checkered dress rolled up above her elbows. He thought he'd never hear enough of a woman's skirt tails swishing as she walked. "Dinner ready?" he asked past the lump in his throat.

"Yes, the children were all getting washed up so I came to get you. Need help?" she asked.

Yes, but not the kind you are willing to give, he thought. "No, I can walk that far. Look at all this tack I've worked on." He motioned toward the job he'd done. "Maybe I'll take care of what's in your stable tomorrow. It's good exercise. And Violet, if you don't want dogs on your place it's all right. Jimmy can keep Molly here until I get ready to leave."

"Are you trying to talk me out of my dog, Orrin Wilde?" She raised an eyebrow.

"No, it's just that the house is yours, it's not mine, and I had no place being so bullish," he said.

"And I had no business being so tacky. Now, that's as much apologizing as either one of us is going to do. Probably ever. Let's go eat dinner and take our babies home. I can't have a child, so I guess a brown dog will have to do," she said.

"You can't have children? I'm so sorry. You would make a fine mother," he said, his voice catching somewhere in his chest. Poor, poor Violet. Life had treated her miserably.

"I can have children, Orrin. Zeb couldn't. And I think it's frowned upon if a woman has a child with no husband. Dinner is getting cold. The girls worked hard on a big pot of pinto beans and fried potatoes. They've even made up a batch of Emma's ginger cakes. You haven't lived until you've eaten ginger cakes." Violet started out of the barn without even looking back to see if he was following her.

"Did we just have a conversation without fighting?" he asked incredulously as he walked beside her toward the house.

"Yes, but don't expect it to ever happen again," she said. "You only get one miracle in your life. And you've had two in less than ten days. You're alive, and we spent five minutes talking without fighting."

"Yes, ma'am," he said with a grin. Maybe he would talk to Jed some more about that land after all. Maybe miracles, like accidents, came in sets of three. If so, he was due one more—and Orrin Wilde knew exactly what he wanted it to be.

Chapter Nine

Orrin polished tack. He straightened the stables. He played with the dogs. He thought. He fretted. Deep down in his soul he knew he'd found his place and it wasn't in Blue Ridge, Texas. The thought of leaving Logan County, Oklahoma, bewildered him. He couldn't ask Jed to help him buy the land because it would break Violet's heart. She'd feel betrayed by her best friends. That left only one option, and rejection terrified him.

Violet figured her days with Orrin were numbered now that he could spend his hours in the stables. It wouldn't be long until he could pick up that saddle and put it on Coaly's back. When that day arrived, he'd ride out of Dodsworth without even looking back. She did laundry. She ironed. She cooked. She thought about ways to keep him in Oklahoma. She thought about moving back to Texas. She fretted.

Scrub oak trees were just silhouettes as the sun set behind them in a blaze of orange glory. The new mint green leaves were no longer visible when Orrin sucked in a lung full of air and started toward the house. His whole future lay in her answer to his question. Either he would disappear in the darkness like those trees when the sun had fully vanished. Or he'd stay and try to start all over with Violet. Talk about asking God for a miracle.

He squared his shoulders as he opened the back door. The poignant aroma of fresh baked gingerbread filled the kitchen. A pot of rabbit stew bubbled on the back burner and Violet was just setting a pan of hot biscuits on the warmer. A wisp of hair stuck to the sweat on her forehead and there was a smudge of flour on the end of her nose. Orrin had never seen a more beautiful woman than Violet was right then. When he left her behind in Texas, she'd been a tall, handsome girl. But the past eight years had matured her into a beauty that just plumb took his breath away.

"Smells good in here," he said.

"Wash up and we'll eat." She didn't even look up from the stove. The table was already set. Coffee was simmering on the back burner to go with the peach cobbler for dessert. Violet would miss Orrin when he left. There was something that satisfied a woman's soul when she cooked for a man with a healthy appetite.

He bowed his head for the grace she offered and then waited for her to ladle the soup into the bowls. Carrots and potatoes cooked to perfection with chunks of rabbit so tender they practically melted in his mouth. He waited until she had eaten a few bites before his courage built enough to present her with the idea.

"You been pretty quiet lately," she said.

He nodded. "Been thinking."

"Oh, no. That gets you in trouble." She blew on the spoonful of soup.

"Violet, I know you got some land for sale. That hundred and sixty that Zeb got in the land run. You know I've got money, and I want to buy that land. I'll pay you the fair price for it. Just name it, and we'll go to the bank tomorrow and take it out of that account your friend set up over there." He talked fast and tried to read her face. It was impossible. She just stared at him with the blankest look he'd ever seen. He put another bite into his mouth. It tasted like sawdust mixed with some kind of tomatoes. He chewed and chewed and had to swallow twice to get it down.

"Why on earth would you want my land?" she finally asked. Coldness dripped off her words like long icicles from the eave of a house in December.

"I like it here in this part of the country. Like you said, all our people have left Blue Ridge. Momma is over in Leonard. Daddy died last year. Jed told me Monday when we were over there that you had that parcel of land you were trying to sell. Said it was about the same kind of land he's got. That's what I want," Orrin said.

A million thoughts went through her mind. Having him so close would be a nightmare. He didn't want anything to do with a widow. Especially Zeb's widow. She remembered what he said about Zeb being bald and ten years older than they were. He'd never want a relationship with the woman who'd married Zeb and lived with him seven years as his wife.

Then again, she did want to sell the land, and Orrin's money was as good as anyone else's. At a time when most folks were struggling just to make the improvements on their claims so they could eventually get a clear title, Orrin could pay cash for the land and build anything he wanted on it. But could she bear to see him take another woman to a brand new house? Tears formed in the back of her eyes and it took every bit of her self will to keep them from flowing down her cheeks.

Zeb rode a horse with all those other people to claim that section of land. He ate dust, waited in line to register his claim. Talked about the whole experience like it was the one star in the universe of his existence. Someday the two of them were going to build a house on that land back before he died. Wouldn't it be like sacrilege to sell it to Orrin Wilde? Zeb would rise up out of that grave in the church yard and haunt her if he ever found out that Orrin Wilde had a clear title to his property.

"Zeb is dead. What do *you* want?" Emma's words came back to her. But this was more than deciding to have a dog on her place. Yet, was it? Zeb didn't like dogs. Zeb was dead. That part of her life was gone forever. She was alive. What did she want? The question could be answered in two words. But she didn't trust Orrin. Might never be able to trust him again. That's the way marriage was spelled. T-R-U-S-T. Without it there was a union but no unity.

"Well, I guess that caught you by surprise," Orrin finally said. "You don't have to give me an answer right now. I can wait a couple of days." Even waiting would be better than the out and out, final no, he read on her face as she paused, spoon halfway to her mouth without saying a word. Her gray eyes had no life in them, and she scarcely breathed.

"I can't imagine you living in Dodsworth, Oklahoma, is all." She finally put the soup in her mouth.

I can't imagine living anywhere else, he thought. "I like it here. Folks are friendly and neighborly. Kind of like Blue Ridge when we were kids."

"Well, I'll give it some thought," she said.

Before he could answer, someone knocked on the front door. Orrin pushed his chair back slightly so he could see through the kitchen door and across the living room. Whoever it was, Violet didn't swing open the door and invite them right in. He didn't recognize the man's voice, but he could hear him plainly.

"Evening, Violet. I've come about that parcel of land you've got for sale out there by Jed and Emma's place. A man come into the bank today askin' about a place to buy.

Said he had money to pay cash and I told him about the land. He said he'd be comin' by to see you about it tomorrow. Tall fellow. Blonde hair. Swedish looking, I'm thinkin'. Anyway, Anna Marie got a burr in her saddle to come to Dodsworth tonight and see her Momma. You know Anna Marie. There ain't no tellin' her no, so here we are. Just thought I'd stop by and tell you that this fellow is comin' to talk to you. Name is Ivan Svenson. If you've changed your mind I'll tell him about the hundred and sixty over to the west of town. But thought I'd give you first chance at his money."

"Well, thank you Alford. I've been tryin' to sell that property for a year. I'll look forward to visitin' with Mr. Svenson," Violet said. "We are just sitting to supper. Would you like to come in and have a bite with us?"

"No, got to get on down to the preacher's house. Anna Marie and her Momma are cooking up something. Sure smells good in there though. Cobbler?" Alford asked.

"Yes. Emma's recipe, with a little dash of cinnamon. Want to have some to hold you 'til supper?" she asked.

"Wouldn't dare. Anna Marie would smell it on my breath and she'd have a fit. She said I wasn't even to set foot inside your living room. Got this big notion about that man who you been helpin' out. But that's Anna Marie. You know how she is," he said, chuckling.

"Well, thanks for coming by," Violet said. "I'll think on selling that land to your Mr. Svenson. Do you think he'd make a good neighbor to the Thomas family?"

"Pretty hardworking Swede from what I could see. Calluses on his big hands. And talked about coming from a farming family," Alford said as he disappeared into the dark night.

Orrin turned his hands over to check for calluses. There'd been a ridge of them across his palms when he'd panned for gold every day. He remembered those first days at the mine when the blisters popped up. He'd just lost his chance at that land. It was as plain as the moon shining out the kitchen window. He should have asked a couple of days ago when the notion first came to him. By now she would have either said yes or no. Now she had a chance to sell it to a big old Swede, so Orrin wouldn't ever get it. However, that Alford had mentioned something about another piece of land out west of Dodsworth. He wouldn't be neighbors with Jed and Emma, but he would at least have a place close to the town.

"Guess you heard that?" She sat back down and stirred her soup. Steam still rose from the top of it so she blew on the first spoonful. "Land has laid there for a year and suddenly I've got two folks wanting it."

"Well, I guess you'll have to meet with the Swede and see who you want Emma and Jed to have for neighbors," he said. It came out sharper than he intended, almost like an accusation.

"Are you saying I'm playing God?" she challenged.

"Not at all. Just that I offered to buy it first. Whatever you are asking I'll give you more, Violet. Or put it up for auction and let me and the Swede bid on it," Orrin said.

"I'm asking a fair price. You can't influence me with all that gold, Orrin Wilde," she snapped. Why were they fighting again? Just when she thought maybe they could be friends he got all bull-headed and edgy.

"I'm going out to the stables and play with my dog." He threw his napkin on the table and stormed out the back door.

"Don't you dare touch my dog. I don't want her to know you," Violet raised her voice so it reached him halfway across the back yard. He sure could move fast when he was angry. Maybe he'd just ride away right then and forget about the land. If so, then she'd stand on the porch and rejoice. She might even dance a jig around the rose bush just to let the whole town know how happy she was to be back in her own world. One without Orrin Wilde in the middle of it.

"She already likes me better than you. Matter of fact, she's going to cry for me when I leave here on Monday." He tossed the bitter words over his shoulder and kept walking. Now what on earth had made him say he was leaving on Monday? He had no intentions of leaving Dodsworth, and to leave Violet's house on Monday? That was only three days away. But now that he'd said it, he'd have to live with it. He surely did hope that Jed was serious about letting him live in that little cabin on his property. If not, well, he'd lived under the stars before. He could do it again.

"You aren't taking my dog anywhere." She slammed the back door behind her and before he could turn around she was just inches from his face.

"Oh, go back in the house and do women's work and leave me alone," he said.

"Don't you order me around, Orrin Wilde," she yelled, shoving her forefinger in his chest with each word. "You're just a little boy in a big man's body. If you can't have your way about that land, then you'll just take your toys and go home."

He grabbed her hand and held it tightly. As usual, just the touch of her skin against his made his heart skip a beat or two. "I'm not acting any more childish than you are, Violet Daniels."

"Violet McDonald. I haven't been Violet Daniels since you walked out on me, Orrin." She jerked her hand away from his and shoved both her hands into her apron pockets. "Katy is my dog and you're not taking her anywhere with you, and that's a fact."

"Are we arguing about dogs or what?" Orrin asked.

"What else would we fight about? Anything else we shared died a long time ago. Now go on out there and do whatever you big masculine men do when you lose a fight with a woman. Lick your wounds or kick something. But don't you bring that surly attitude back into my house."

"Your house. Your dog. Until you get ready to share, you won't ever have anyone in your life, Violet," he said.

"Well, they'll sell homemade ice cream at the gates of Hades before I share anything in my life with you. I'm going in the house and do my woman things, now, because you aren't worth fighting with." She turned around with flair and took her anger right back inside the house. She kicked the rag rug in front of the dry sink and sent it flying across the room. She'd sell her land to Ivan Svenson tomorrow for less money than she'd been asking. She'd make a pact with the devil himself to keep Orrin Wilde from ever living on the land Zeb had owned.

Violet stared at the shifting pattern on the ceiling. Moonlight filtered in through the lace curtains in her bedroom, and as the curtains fanned out with the occasional breeze the patterns moved. She'd made up her mind in the kitchen and hadn't changed it. Orrin Wilde could ride away on Monday and she'd be glad to have him gone. By noon on the same day she hoped to have her land signed over to some tall Swede.

She heard his footsteps in the kitchen and the living room and then the door to the bedroom shut carefully. She hoped he was miserable and disappointed. That he laid there with his hands laced behind his back just like she was doing. But knowing him, he probably went to sleep as soon as his head hit the pillow. The first tear drop hung on her eyelashes; then it slowly traveled down her cheek, leaving a shiny streak of moisture in its wake. That opened up the dam, and Violet cried for the first time in years. She'd been sad at her parent's funerals and at Zeb's, but she hadn't known true misery until that very night. The kind that shatters a woman's heart . . . for the second time.

She buried her face in the pillow so Orrin couldn't hear

her sobs. That's all he'd need to puff up his already inflated ego. To know that the decision she had to live with was so painful that it brought her to her knees. She cried herself into a fitful sleep where she dreamed of days in Blue Ridge when she and Orrin were so much in love.

She held a wet wash cloth on her eyes for several minutes the next morning but it didn't take away the redness, the swelling or the dark circles under her eyes. It didn't magically make the haunted hurt disappear. He'd rustled around in the kitchen and eaten a cold biscuit from supper and was already out at the stables when she went to the kitchen to make breakfast. Well, if he was going to pout all day then she'd take a morning off. She picked up a biscuit and bit into it. She chewed but it was no more than something flaky in her mouth. No flavor. So much like her life would be from that day forth. Nothing to spice it up. Violet McDonald would wallow in her little rut and never again crawl out of it. She'd be that old crazy widow woman who lived in the last house on the south side of Dodsworth. When she died there'd be no children to mourn her going. If Katy outlived her she'd will the dog back to Jimmy, along with all her earthly possessions.

She was still swimming in a self-filled pity pool when someone knocked on the door. It was too early for the Swede to be arriving. Maybe Anna Marie had spent the night and was coming to check on her. *Well, come right on Mrs. High and Mighty. You'll find that Orrin has run away to his little sanctuary and I'm fully dressed, so we didn't sleep together*, she thought as she went to answer the door.

The man was even taller than Orrin and as blond as Orrin was dark. He wore bibbed overalls and sturdy workboots, not unlike what Jim Parsons wore most of the time. He held his straw hat in his hands and smiled brightly at her. "Mrs. McDonald, I'm Ivan Svenson. I hope I'm not too early. I just rode over here from Guthrie. Alford told me he was going to talk to you last night."

"Come inside, Ivan. Don't stand out there on the porch," she said, cordially opening the door for him. "Could I get you a cup of coffee or a glass of water?"

"No, ma'am." Ivan stood just inside the door, as out of place in her living room as a toad frog in a punch bowl. "I just wanted to tell you that . . ."

"Sit down, Mr. Svenson. Please," she said, motioning toward the settee.

He looked out of place perched on the edge of the furniture. "I hope Alford didn't get your hopes up about selling that land. He told me last night when he got home about that other piece over west of town. I drove by it on the way and I really do like that parcel. To be honest it's a little closer to Guthrie and it's a little cheaper on the price. I haven't seen your land yet, but if you've a mind to drive with me out there, then I'll take a look at it still. But I'm thinkin' I'll buy the other one. If I hurry, I might get a little fall wheat in and still put up a cabin for the winter, too," he said.

Violet had the urge to tell Mr. Svenson he could have her land for free—just pay the costs to change the deed—but that would be spiteful. She'd prayed last night when she went to bed for God to give her strength to sell her land to this Swede. And evidently God had said no . . . again. She knew from past experience that it was useless to argue with the Almighty. When He said no, the answer did not ever become yes just because she prayed harder or argued longer.

"Mr. Svenson, I have to admit something to you. When Alford came to ask me about my land and to tell me that you would come calling, I had another person asking me to buy that land right then. I'm glad you like the other piece of property and I hope you'll like Dodsworth. It's a good town, lots of good families here. And we'll welcome you into the town. Do you have a family?"

"No, ma'am," he said, blushing so red it made his hair even blonder. "I'm only twenty years old. I've a mind to take a wife, but I just haven't found the right one yet. Maybe there'll be some nice woman in Dodsworth or Guthrie."

"I'm sure there will be. We'll hope to see you in church real soon if you buy that land. We've got our summer picnic coming up in a few weeks. Folks go to church on Sunday morning, have a picnic and visiting all afternoon, then go for the evening services. Kind of gets a little fellowship in that way. Maybe you'll be settled enough to join us," she said.

"I'll sure hope so. I understand you are a widow woman, Mrs. McDonald," he said, the blush deepening even more.

"I am that," she said. Was this mere boy trying to court her? Well, wouldn't Anna Marie just get a case of pure vapors over that?

"Well, I'll be going now. I'm anxious to get the business done. Would you know who might be my neighbors?" he asked.

"The Listens live on the next farm over from that land. Maggie is their oldest daughter. A tall red-haired girl who loves to dance. Then there's Elenor and Grace, in that order I think," Violet said.

"Well, I can't dance. I got two left feet," he said. Then he jumped up and was out the door with barely a good-bye.

Violet sat in her rocker for several minutes before she finally made herself stand up and go out the back door. She found Orrin sitting on a pile of hay with the two puppies in his lap. His eyes were as swollen as hers and just as dark. He looked up with a mixture of anger and disappointment in his face.

He'd seen the tall, nice-looking man ride up and watched

as he went in the front door. He didn't stay long, so evidently she'd sold him the land and he would be Jed and Emma's neighbor. The rest of the story was written in the stars. Because Ivan Svenson would be their neighbor, they would have him to supper. Because they didn't want him to be lonely, they'd invite Violet to join them.

"Are you spoiling my dog?" she asked.

"Katy is easy to spoil. She's not like some women I know," he said and wished he could bite his tongue off. If nothing else, he should be glad for Violet. Glad that after the way he'd misused her trust that she could find someone else.

"Some women never had a chance to be spoiled. Hitch up the horses. We're going to Guthrie," she said.

"So you can sell your land?" he asked.

"That's right. So I can sell my land. Seems Mr. Svenson liked the other parcel of land so much he's a mind to buy it. We're going to Guthrie so I can sell my land to you, Orrin Wilde. By this time next year you'll be wishing you'd never bought it, but don't come crawling back to me begging me to buy it back."

Could he be asleep and dreaming? Surely she didn't just say she'd sell him that land. "I don't think I'll be changing my mind," he said, unable to keep the grin from his face. "Why did you decide to sell it to me then? You could just keep it."

"You need a place to go on Monday when you get out of my house," she said bluntly.

"Yes, ma'am." He pushed the puppies back and wrapped his arms around her waist, pulling her to his chest for a bear hug. The kiss that came next rocked the earth under them and lit up the morning sky even brighter than the sun. He tasted a little bit of morning coffee, and Heaven. She fit into his arms so naturally that her heart started singing something about belonging there forever. She'd trusted her heart before and just look what that got her. She pulled away him and started through across the barn. Orrin Wilde might steal a kiss . . . or even two . . . but her heart wasn't up for grabs. Not ever again.

"Thanks, Violet," he whispered.

"For the land?"

"For everything," he said, smiling.

"Hmmph," she snorted and went back to the house to change into her best Sunday dress. The woman looking back at her in the mirror had changed in the past few days. Her gray eyes were bright with dots of glitter. High color filled her cheeks. Anyone looking at her would know she was in love.

"Love," she whispered. "I'll always love him. Did from the time we were little kids. But that surely don't mean I could ever trust him again or live with him forever, either."

Chapter Ten

 V iolet surely didn't feel like a sweet little innocent flower that night. Of course, her mother hadn't known Violet would take after the Daniels side of the family and grow up to be anything but a dainty little flower when she'd named her that. She felt more like a giant zinnia in her yellow dress when she walked into the communitywide summer social being held in Jed's barn. She should have sewn herself up something in a soft gray or even a blue, but the yellow fabric looked so inviting in the dressmaker's shop when she'd taken her five dresses in on Thursday. Now she wondered whatever had possessed her, with her height and size, to make herself a sunshine yellow dress.

Tables were set up with every kind of food the women folks could bake or cook the past couple of days. Violet had brought a triple-tiered chocolate cake to add to the menagerie of cookies, pies, hams, baked beans, and potato salads. If anyone went away hungry it would be their own fault. She hoped everyone kept eating and dancing and she could stay hidden in the corner for the whole night. It was the first time she'd been to a social affair since Zeb died, and she felt like the dim light lit up her yellow dress even more.

She'd just about decided to slip out the door, plead a headache if she ran into anyone asking why she was leaving, and go home. She'd already taken a step in that direction when Orrin walked through the double doors in the back of the barn. Her heart stopped beating and then took off like it was propelled with a steam engine. She hadn't seen him since Monday morning when, true to his word, he'd saddled up his black horse, taken his dog, Molly, and rode out of her life. Her dog, Katy, had whined and wiggled in her arms, begging to be let loose so she could run after the other puppy.

"Hush," she'd crooned to Katy. "I know just how you feel, but some things just aren't possible." He'd taken Katy's sister and best friend. He'd taken Violet's heart for the second time in her life. She had taken Katy into the house and started to sew, hoping to forget all about him. It didn't work.

Katy slept on the rug beside the rocking chair and whined at the door when nature called. Katy rode in the seat beside her when Violet took five dresses to the dressmaker in Guthrie on Thursday. All week she'd worked hard at settling back into her daily routine without Orrin. She'd patted herself on the back for a job well done—until she saw him standing in the barn doors. That's when the truth jumped out and stung her. She'd missed him horribly. Missed cooking for him. Missed the arguments. Dreamed about him during her waking hours as well as the long and lonely nights.

"Mrs. McDonald," a soft voice said right over her left shoulder. "Would you care to dance?"

Ivan smiled when she looked back. "I can't do so well,

but if you'd allow me to try a slow dance, I might not ruin your little bitty feet."

Strange, Ivan was the first man who'd noticed that her feet didn't match the rest of her build. There she was inching upon six feet tall, with feet smaller than Anna Marie's. She smiled. "I'd love to dance. I'm not so very good at it, either, so we'll just plod along with each other."

She put one gloved hand on Ivan's shoulder and let him wrap his big hands around her other one. The band members played a slow waltz and Ivan did a fair job of keeping the rhythm. She glanced around the barn to see where Orrin was and saw Maggie sidling right up next to him. Now that would be a match made far from Heaven. Maggie, who didn't care about anything in the world but dancing, and Orrin. Those Wilde brothers, all six of them, could dance circles around anyone in Blue Ridge from the time they were able to stand steady on their own two feet. Maggie might have just met her match, and Orrin might have just met the woman to make him pay for all eternity for his adventure in California. She almost laughed aloud at the thought of Orrin and Maggie spending their lives together. Now that truly would be a union with no unity.

The thought was only funny for a split second; then the smile faded. Orrin with Maggie? Orrin kissing her goodnight like he'd kissed Violet? Jealousy filled her breast so fully that she figured her face was green with it.

"What did you smile about?" Ivan asked.

"Have you met Maggie?" Violet answered the question with another one.

"Yes, ma'am. The Listens asked me over to their house for supper last night. I've got a tent pitched on my land now and I'm making a cabin. Not so big. Just one room with a sleeping loft for now. Maybe later I can add on to it," he said, blushing again.

"Did you like Maggie?" Violet asked. They'd make a cute couple. Him with his blonde hair and towering height.

Maggie with that red unruly mop of hair and her flighty ways. She'd keep him from being so staid. He'd clip her wings and give her some stability.

"I do not like that girl," Ivan declared without so much as a hint of a grin. "She is your friend and my neighbor so I do not want to hurt your feelings any more than your toes . . . but Maggie isn't really all there, is she? She's interested in dancing and likes to talk about the next time she can dance. No, Mrs. McDonald, I do not like Maggie. When I find a wife, she will have to be stable."

"I see." Violet smiled. Were widow women past their prime stable enough for Ivan Svenson?

Maggie said something to Orrin and he nodded. They stepped onto the straw dance section of the barn and the band started up a fast reel. Everyone else stood back and let them have center stage. Orrin kept up with her so well that her eyes glistened. Violet slipped away from the audience and went outside for a breath of air. She found Emma sitting on the back of a wagon with Lalie Joy in her arms.

"Yellow is good on you, Violet. You should wear it often. I'm glad you're out of those blacks and grays you wore in mourning. Did I see that young Swedish lad dancing with you?" Emma asked.

"Yes, you did. I'm afraid I'll have to be careful. I think he would like me to be a stable wife for him," Violet said, laughing.

"He's too young for you, Violet," Emma said. "Would you hold the baby for a spell? She's finished nursing now, and I'd like to claim my husband for a dance before Maggie gets hold of him and I won't have a chance."

"I'd be glad to." Violet opened her arms, and Emma laid the baby in them. "But don't worry about Maggie. She's got Orrin roped. The way he can dance I bet before the night is finished, she'll have him branded and hollering for Preacher Elgin to bring his Bible."

"How would you feel about that?" Emma asked.

"I don't know," Violet said, barely above a whisper. "Jealous if I'm honest. But it don't seem to matter none anyway. Orrin blew up the relationship we had way back eight years ago. I'm not so sure I'd ever trust him again. And besides, all we do is fight."

Emma buttoned the front of her light blue dress trimmed in lace. "Well, fighting is a good start. You can always spend some time making up if you fight. Come on inside and listen to the music at least. Lalie Joy loves the music."

"I can't believe you are already back in your clothes and Lalie Joy is only a few weeks old." Violet followed her back into the barn. "And that blue is so good on you, Emma. Jed probably can't keep his eyes off you."

"It ain't his eyes that I'm worried about," Emma said. "Have you seen the new patterns? There's one that would make up beautiful in ivory brocade if you was to ever let one of these fellers propose."

"That's enough of that kind of talk," Violet said, and shook her head.

Orrin could have shot that tall blonde Swede right between the eyes when he saw him lead Violet out onto the dance floor. Orrin had dressed with care and looked forward to seeing her again, even hoped to dance with her. To start a courtship that all the men in the county would recognize and back away from the widow McDonald. But there was that kid horning in on his business. He'd asked Maggie to dance with him just to get back at Violet, and it was backfiring rapidly. The girl could dance. He had to give her that much. All that gorgeous red hair and that swishy dress. But then it didn't take him five minutes to know the distance between her ears was as empty as a shallow creek in a drought. Maggie Listen danced wonderfully, but that was the extent of her abilities.

When the second dance ended he pleaded old age, to the laughter of the whole audience, and went to the punch bowl for a drink. But mostly to scan the barn and find Violet. Maggie had started a slow dance with Jim Parsons, who looked somewhat like a bear dancing with a ballerina. Jed and Emma were hugged up together, looking deep into each other's eyes. That's what Orrin wanted in a woman. Someone like Emma. *Someone like Violet*, his heart said flatly. Yes, he agreed, but Violet could never love him again. Not with the past lurking around ruining the present as well as the future. He located her sitting in the corner holding Emma's new baby. Sarah sat on one side of her and Mary on the other. They were laughing and talking. An aching pang of desire clutched his heart. What he wanted more than anything else in the world was to talk to Violet and make her eyes sparkle.

Ivan spotted Violet at the same time Orrin did. He wandered over to where she sat with the children and pulled up a chair to sit with them. About the time he sat down, Jim Parsons noticed that someone else was interested in Violet. He decided right then he would forgive her for having a man in her house. If Preacher Elgin didn't find fault with her and if the women in the community hadn't shunned her over her Christian deed, then perhaps Jim had been a little hasty. Violet would still make him a good steady wife. They might even raise up a boy or two to help him on his land. She was a little long in the tooth but that didn't mean she couldn't birth a few children before she died.

Jim made his way through the people to the chair Sarah had vacated when she ran outside with another little girl with long braids. No doubt they'd be practicing their dance steps so that in a few years they'd know what to do when a fellow asked them to dance. He sat down beside Violet, who suddenly felt smothered by all the people around her.

"Evening, Violet. Reckon I could beg a dance. Bet Miss Mary here could hold that baby for you. Is that Emma's new daughter? Right pretty little thing, ain't she?" Jim said.

Violet was in shock. Jim Parson's voice actually had a bit of life to it when he looked at the baby. "I suppose we might. But wouldn't that be pretty dangerous ground for you, Jim? Wouldn't want all these young girls to be thinking you are interested in someone with my reputation."

"Guess I was wrong about that," Jim said. "But I'm not wrong about this. I don't cotton to a woman with a bunch of sass in her. So I'll just leave you alone now. I was thinking on forgiving you, but I'm changing my mind. Don't know what happened when that man lived with you, but I don't like it. You've changed, Violet McDonald. You didn't used to be so quick to smart off. I don't like it. Good night, Violet."

Ivan looked at Violet like she had horns sprouting from her dark hair. "You lived with a man, did you?"

"Yes, she did," Mary piped right up. "Someone shot him and he fell right on her doorstep with a big ugly bleeding wound on his back. They slept together for two or three weeks and then he moved out. They had a big fight but they haven't gone to the bedroom yet since they had the fight. When they do, they'll come out all happy and he'll kiss her and it will all be fine."

Ivan's blue eyes widened in disbelief that a little girl would talk like that. He fumbled for words and finally simply said he was going to find someone to dance with and disappeared.

Violet burst into a fit of giggles as soon as he was out of hearing range, and Mary put her hands on her hips and demanded to know just what she'd said that made the pretty man so angry. "All I did was tell the truth. That's the way Momma and Daddy Jed do when they have a fight. They go to the bedroom and we can hear them hollerin', then they stay a little while after it quiets down. Then they come out and Daddy Jed kisses her and everything is all right. He's whistling and she's humming."

"But Mary, I didn't sleep with Orrin," Violet said.

"Well, I didn't mean that you slept with him in his bed. I meant that you both slept in the same house. That Ivan sure is a stupid old ox of a man if he don't understand any better than that. And here I was thinkin' I might like him when I grow up and get ready to marry up with a fellow and have fights of my own," she said.

"Let's hope you find a fellow you don't have to fight with. One who'll drop down on his knees every morning and offer up thanks that he's got you for a wonderful wife," Violet said.

"One like Orrin," Mary said, dreamily. "If he wasn't in love with you, I'd make him wait on me to grow up."

Violet was too stunned for words.

"Well, now what did I say? That's all we hear when Orrin eats lunch with us. He's been helping Daddy Jed with the chores to build up his arms and to pay for the cabin he's livin' in so he eats lunch with us most days. We hear Violet this and Violet that all the time."

"Is that right?" Violet finally said.

"You ready to trade?" Emma was suddenly in the circle with them again, reaching for her child. "You dance a while, and I'll play with this baby doll."

"Sounds like a poor trade to me," Violet said smiling, but handed the baby to her.

"Would you care to dance?" Orrin stepped from behind Emma. He'd watched the two men leave her side and wondered what had been said.

"Of course she wants to dance," Mary said. "I'd dance with you if I was old enough but since I'm too young, you'll just have to dance with Violet. Besides, Jim and Ivan done ran off when I said she'd been sleeping with you only I didn't mean it like that, I meant you two had been sleeping in the same house and anyway they ran off so you need to dance with her."

"Violet?" Orrin's eyes were dancing with laughter.

"I'm a marked woman with a reputation so if I want to dance, it'd better be with you, I guess," she said.

"Mary, did you really say that?" Emma was aghast.

"Sorry Momma. I just got my story all messed up that time, didn't I? Well, I'm going out and practice dancing with Sarah and the girls." Mary raced off out the door.

"I'm sorry, Violet." Emma giggled.

"I'm not. Tell Mary I owe her one special dress. She took care of two problems I didn't want to deal with." Violet took Orrin's hand and let him lead her out to the dance floor.

"So tell me about the California gold business," she said as they danced a slow waltz together.

"In one word. Lonely. Didn't see another soul for weeks on end. Just panned gold and did a little digging. This is like Heaven for me, Violet. People to talk to and neighbors. It's like home." He kept her at a proper arm's length. No use in making tongues wag any more than they already had. Besides, Mary had a knack of telling outlandish stories without any provocation. No telling what would happen if he drew Violet close to him for a waltz.

She wanted to snuggle right down into his chest. Had he really talked about her that much, or was Mary fabricating more tales? If he had, then she wondered if maybe they could start all over again and build a new relationship. It was a crazy thought right there in the middle of Jed and Emma's barn dance, but it stuck in her heart.

"Guess those two men are interested in the widow McDonald's newly acquired money," he said.

"You mean, you don't think they could be interested in me?" She glared at him.

"Seems to me like you're always looking for something to get mad at me about," he said.

"I don't have to look far," she retorted.

"Take a walk with me to get some fresh air," he said, stopping in the middle of the dance.

"I don't think so, Orrin. You know what that means. It means we could be courting. And I don't intend to let people think that," she said, without moving an inch.

"We lived together in your house and you didn't care what people thought. Mary told your suitors that we slept together, and you just laughed. But you won't take a simple walk out in the night air with me?" he asked.

"Let's just sit over there in that corner and talk," she suggested.

"That won't ruin your already tainted reputation, will it?" His voice was cold and icy.

"Probably, since it's with a rogue like you, but I'll chance it." She dropped his hand from hers. If he followed her to the corner, they might talk. If he didn't, so be it. She didn't need Orrin in her life anymore. *Oh yes you do*, her heart singsonged at that absurd thought.

"Now what did you want to talk about?" she asked when she'd gotten comfortable sitting in one of the kitchen chairs Emma had brought from the house to the barn.

"Us," he said, simply.

"Orrin, there is no us. We have grown up and apart. What we had was just a foundation that never got built on. It's crumbled and fallen with the storms of life. It's not worth building anything on now," she said, sadly.

"Can we forget the past and start a new foundation?" he asked.

"Are you asking me if you can court me?" she asked right back.

"I'm asking you if we could be friends. And yes, I guess I am asking you if I could court you," he said.

A cold chill traveled down her spine in spite of the hot night air. He'd laid it on the line and she didn't have an answer. "I don't know," she whispered.

"Well, you think on it a few days. I'm not in any hurry. I've got a house to get up before winter sets in and an unforgiving chunk of land to put to the plow when my back is finally healed up enough to take it," he said, smiling.

"What if I say no?" she asked.

"Then I'll just have to live with that answer," he said.

"My Orrin, my Orrin, you have to come and dance with me. My Emma says it's time for little girls to be in bed and I've got to go to the house. But you promised that you would dance with me," Molly interrupted, running and jumping into his arms.

"And I shall," he said, picking her up and carrying her out to the floor. He put one of her small arms around his neck and held the other one straight out as he spun her around in a fast waltz. She giggled and looked at him through the eyes of innocent love. He'd make an excellent father, Violet thought as she watched him with Molly. He should marry a younger woman. At twenty-six a woman should be finishing up with having babies, not just starting a family.

"Eulalie was past thirty," Emma said softly as she sat down beside Violet.

"How did you know what I was thinking?" Violet asked.

"I know you. You are my best friend. Orrin Wilde is a good man. Good with kids. Hard worker. But he's already broken your heart, so you have to be the one to decide about him," Emma said.

"I think what I need is to get away from the forest for a little while. He's got some kind of notion about me because I doctored him back to health. Kind of an obligation thing, I suppose," Violet said.

"Could be. Somehow I don't think so. I thought Jed had an obligation to me and was in love with Anna Marie. That's why I got away from the forest and went home. I'm glad Aunt Beulah could see farther away than I could. Remember she sent me a telegram saying that Molly was dying." Emma giggled.

"I remember." Violet laughed with her. "But this whole

thing just plumb scares me witless. I'm not a young innocent girl anymore, Emma. I've been married, even if it
wasn't the best of situations."

"You think Orrin is a young innocent boy?" Emma widened her blue eyes.

"I never thought about that," Violet whispered.

"My Emma, did you see us dancing? My Orrin held me
up and danced me all over the place. I can't wait until I'm
big enough to dance with a good-looking man like my Orrin," Molly yelled across the barn as Orrin carried her back
to where Violet and Emma sat.

"Remember what I asked you the other night? What do
you want? If you think there's still a chance for you two,
then try a little courtship. If you don't, then you're still my
best friend, Violet," Emma said in hushed tones before the
two mismatched dancers got to them.

"Thank you," Violet said.

"So could we dance again?" Orrin asked Violet.

"Do you think the people won't be saying that you're
dancing with me just to get your money back on the land
you purchased?" she asked.

"Frankly, Violet, I don't care what anyone in this whole
barn thinks. Kind of like you in that matter. Seems like
some folks thought you should just throw my carcass out
in the street so you wouldn't ruin your reputation," he said
with a grin.

"Seems like we fight better than anything else." Again
she let him lead her out on the dance floor.

"Seems that way right now. Might not seem that way
forever though," he said, his mouth aching to kiss her
again.

The firelight flickered off the yellow in her dress as they
danced together. Two souls trying to find the missing half.
Two hearts trying desperately to fall in love again. One
mind that couldn't trust the man. One mind that wanted the
dance to go on and on, so the woman wouldn't leave his
arms.

Chapter Eleven

Violet shut her eyes tightly and tried to will herself to sleep. Katy whimpered and kicked a hind leg on the rug beside the bed; evidently she wasn't having a good night either. Violet mumbled under her breath, "If I can't sleep I might as well get up and make a pot of hot tea." Then she shook her head. No, she wouldn't give in to the insomnia. She picked up her pillow and beat it into the right shape. It didn't offer one bit more comfort when she laid her head back down on it.

She sighed loudly and watched the moon rise out the bedroom window. The night was close and sticky with humidity. Summer had arrived in Indian Territory, and the heat was the cause of her sleeplessness. *Sure it is*, her heart argued, and she frowned at that niggling little voice that seemed to have something to say about everything these days. She finally swung her legs over the side of the bed and opened the window. Maybe she could coax a breeze through the lacy curtains. Until then, she'd use the time to sort out her feelings. To make her crazy heart realize there was no future with a man like Orrin Wilde. No matter how much his touch or his kiss had affected her. He'd said he wanted to court her again, to build a new foundation. Was that even possible? True, he made her heart pound a little harder; filled her with something akin to magical dust that made her float among the clouds when he was around. However, he'd had the same effect on her all those years ago, and when it came right down to the final day, he'd disappeared. Without a note. Without a single letter from his precious gold mine. Would he do the same thing again?

She was still pondering the questions when her eyes got heavy. Mental exhaustion from worry joined with physical exhaustion from trying to outwork the fears to finally claim the tense body of the widow Violet. Deep sleep wasn't far away when she dropped her hand off the side of the bed and rubbed Katy's soft fur one more time. One moment she was reminding herself again of the humiliation she'd faced in Blue Ridge when Orrin didn't show up at the church; the next she was asleep. She dreamed about waiting beside the edge of a creek. The sun was warm on her face and the grass soft on the backs of her bare legs. Orrin would be there in a little while. They'd made arrangements at church on Sunday morning. It was halfway between his parent's farm and her parent's place. A tall oak tree shaded part of the pond. Violet scooted her body over to put her face and arms in the shade. Her mother would fuss for weeks if she brought home a face full of freckles so close to her wedding day. To be truthful, Violet was self-conscious enough about her height than to want to add freckles to the problem. She trailed her hand in the cool water and smiled, thinking of the next week when Orrin would wait for her at the front of the church.

She laid back and shut her eyes while she waited. Orrin must have gotten behind in his chores to be so late. She'd barely gotten comfortable under the shade tree when she heard a rustling in the brush and the whiff of a skunk wafted through the air. Her nostrils flared in disgust. Now wouldn't that just be a horror. To smell like a rotten old skunk on her wedding day. She sat up slowly and wrapped her arms around her long legs, making sure her dress covered her ankles. The sound of a puppy's soft yapping came through the brush. Orrin's dog must be following him. Good grief! They'd both smell like skunk if that black and white critter raised his tail and started stomping the earth. She remembered the time her brother came home smelling like a skunk. Her mother had tried vinegar and practically bathed him in tomato juice. Nothing worked very well. He'd told them that when the skunk felt threatened it stomped the ground and then raised its tail high in the air. Seemed he'd been too slow by the time the latter was in effect, and the skunk had gotten him good. Violet inhaled deeply. The smell was still there but it wasn't just like her brother had smelled for days and days. It was a rancid, sickening odor that made her want to hold her breath, but it wasn't a skunk. More like something died back under the brush and the buzzards hadn't kept their contract with Mother Nature.

Orrin's puppy began to yip in earnest. Maybe she'd just forgotten the exact way they smelled. The dog was probably chasing the skunk back through the brush. She heard Orrin's soft laughter in the background. What exactly was funny about skunks? Men! She'd never understand them even if she was desperately, hopelessly in love with one. Strange, though, it seemed like that stupid pup was running the skunk closer to her rather than chasing him away. The smell just kept getting stronger and stronger and the puppy's yelps were nearer and nearer to her ear.

"And now it is time for you to wake up, giant lady," Orrin said with a funny accent. How dare him call her a giant lady. He knew she was sensitive about being so tall, and he'd always said he thought she was beautiful even though she was almost six feet tall. She twisted her head around, looking for him to appear though the brush any second. She remembered sitting up and wrapping her arms around her knees, but suddenly in the fantasy world of dream she was lying on her back, staring at the leaves on the trees again. She started to sit up but some kind of vicious ivy had wrapped itself around her arm and bound her to the oak tree. She pulled against it but it wouldn't let go. Her arm was drawn so tightly that it ached, but she couldn't break the ivy tendrils. Orrin would take care of it when he finally stopped laughing about his dog and arrived at her side. He'd take out his knife and cut the ivy away and then rub her wrist for a while until it stopped chaffing.

"Wake up, woman," Orrin demanded with the same silly accent. He liked to play games, but this wasn't the time. She wanted loose from the ivy. She wanted to sit up and wrap her arms around his neck and steal a kiss. She mumbled his name and the noise of it leaving her mouth almost woke her from the dream. But she couldn't wake up yet, not until he'd freed her from the vine.

She strained against the tenacious tendrils. This wasn't funny. Orrin had better get his pocket knife out and cut her loose soon or he was going to get a piece of her mind he didn't want. Then even in her sleep she knew she was dreaming. It was just a silly dream. Violet forced her eyelids to open and see just what it was that Katy was having such a fit about.

"Ah, so the giant woman is going to wake up after all," the man chuckled. He sat on the end of her bed and stared at her with evil black eyes. Katy had been tied to the foot board of the bed. She barked at the man and strained at the short rope around her neck.

For a moment, Violet didn't think she'd left the foggy world of dreamland and really opened her eyes. She started to sit up and found that one arm was tied securely to one of the railings on the iron bedstead. She jerked against it and swiped at the man with the other hand, missing him by more than a foot.

"The giant has a temper." He laughed, showing bad teeth and spraying the air with rancid breath. "But she will learn that it is not wise to mess with Damian. You did something with my gold, woman. By now I'm sure it is already gone since the man, Orrin, is gone. But no one makes a fool of Damian. He got my gold. I shall repay him by taking his woman."

Violet's gray eyes widened in sheer horror. "He will kill you," she said evenly.

"Maybe, but he will have to come to Mexico. Damian is on his way home, and he rides like the devil he is. Santos thought we should take you with us, but I don't want to slow down, and besides, I don't like the big women. Especially one who looks so much like a man. I can't make myself kiss a man." He laughed again. "No, I will not take you with us even for sport for the other three. I'm going to make a sacrifice of you. Your Orrin will find you tomorrow morning in a pile of ashes. Only you are not a magical bird. You will not rise from the ashes to fly with him through the air again. You won't even dance with him again like you did in the barn last week. I thought maybe I would shoot both of you then. But that wouldn't get me the gold. That gold is gone from my hands forever. So I will take what Orrin Wilde cherishes the most. I will take his woman and sacrifice her to the devil himself. Your noisy dog is tied on the bed with you, you will notice. You are tied to the bed, too. I am leaving, now, lady. Say your prayers and ask your God to receive your spirit, because you are about to die."

"You are a wicked . . ." Violet sputtered.

"And you are the same as a dead woman," Damian said, bending to crawl out the window onto the porch. A billow of black smoke filled the room even as he spoke. "Your stables are the first to go. The horses, I will take with me.

I could never kill a good horse. That would be a sin." He was all the way out the window before he stuck his head back inside. "Because you are such a spunky woman, I will make it easier on you. After all, dead is dead, and there won't be enough left to know if you have a bullet hole in your head or not. I have poured enough kerosene in this house to make it go quickly." He tossed a small pistol on the bed. "One bullet. Kill the dog if you can't stand to see it die. Or yourself if you are selfish. Or waste the shot on one attempt to hit me. The choice is yours, giant woman," he said, just before he tossed a match into the bedroom.

The fire sprang up as if it were truly coming from the bowels of Hades. Great flames eating the rug beneath the bed and spreading like a roaring river as it traveled into the living room. Katy howled in fright and Violet grabbed the gun. The man had suggested she shoot either herself or the dog, but Violet didn't intend to do either. She heard the thunder of horse hooves as Damian rode away, so shooting him was out of the question. She tugged at the rope holding her fast to the iron bed which was beginning to glow red with the sudden heat. Sweat popped out all over her body as she aimed the gun toward the rope and pulled the trigger. The bullet severed the rope and she yanked herself free. It took at least a minute to untangle the knot holding Katy, and then she stood up in the middle of the bed, her head brushing the ceiling. Fire ringed the bed and was already running up the curtains on the window where Damian had escaped. One brief look into the living room told her that the whole room was already engulfed. A wall of red blazes separated her from the window—but it was the only chance she had. She picked up the blanket from the bed and wrapped it around herself and Katy. In the next two seconds she tried to prepare herself for the way the fire would burn her feet, but nothing came close to the pain that tore at her body when her bare feet hit the burning wood of the floor. The flames reached out as she ran through the hot coals toward the window, and licked at the trailing tail of the blanket. By the time she threw herself out the open window, even the tail of her nightgown was on fire. She held Katy tightly as she crossed the porch, which was even hotter than the floor of her bedroom. Then she threw the blanket away from them and hit the soft grass in the front yard, rolling and rolling, trying to get the red hot fury away from the bottom of her thin cotton gown.

Katy was frantic with fear, running from Violet to the edge of the porch and back again. Finally, through the frightful edges of pain and the heavy smoke billowing just above her head, Violet began to crawl toward the back yard. Visions of the pond at the back of her property were all that kept her crawling. Her nails broke as she dug them into the dirt and pulled her body along. She couldn't stand on her feet, not even to get to the pond. Katy ran ahead of her, barking and encouraging her to keep crawling.

After an eternity, she felt water on her fingertips and knew she'd made it to the edge of the water. It took forever to turn her body around. She got her blistered feet into the cool water of the pond and thought she heard the water sizzle with the heat just before she passed completely out with the pain. She shuddered one time and a bright white light beckoned her from somewhere other than earth. As she looked into it, the pain ebbed and she found herself floating, her feet not quite touching the ground, toward the peace she could see just ahead.

Orrin was fast asleep, Missy curled up in a fluffy ball at his bedside, when the thump awoke them at the same time. Missy set up a running yelp through the house, scratching at the front door and carrying on like she was going to kill something or someone if Orrin would just open the door.

"Okay, okay, Missy Molly," he said. He stooped down and petted the dog. Whatever had woke him had brought her out of a deep sleep, also. So the thump hadn't been part of a dream after all. "Quiet now, Missy," he whispered. The dog had actually been christened Miss Molly. But calling her Molly caused too much confusion with Jed and Emma's little girl named the same thing. So they'd talked about it for a while and he and Molly decided that Missy would be a good name for the animal.

"It was just a clap of thunder," he said, reassuring the pup as well as himself. "But we'll check it out before we go back to bed." He opened the door just in time to see the rider on the back of a dark horse top the rise in the near distance and to hear the cackle of laughter.

Missy tore out of the house and after the horse, but it was gone before she could scarcely make it across the yard. Orrin's dark eyebrows drew down in a frown. "What was that all about?" he wondered out loud. He whistled for Missy to return and waited for the dog. He scratched his head and yawned and then looked up at the sky. The sun was coming up, making a red glow in the distance. Stars still dotted the sky so it would be a while before it was fully risen.

Missy pranced back to the porch but stopped on the top step. Her hackles rose down her backbone and a low growl started in her throat. She tiptoed around the smelly animal on the porch. It wasn't one of those black and white creatures that came around the barn at night. And it wasn't one of the big rat things either. It wasn't even alive but it did have a horrible smell and hadn't been on the porch when she and her friend went into the house to sleep.

"What is it, girl?" Orrin bowed down to look out into the darkness again. Something wasn't right. He could feel the danger just like he could the night those bandits shot him. He could almost smell the one they called Damian standing on his front porch. The wind shifted and blew something resembling smoke into his nostrils. He looked back at the sun and realized why it appeared so strange.

The sun didn't come up in the west and that wasn't the morning sun ball; it was fire.

"Violet," he mumbled when he realized the fire was near Dodsworth. He jerked himself to a standing position and stumbled over a set of saddlebags that Missy was sniffing all around. He reached down to touch them and all the pieces to the strange puzzle suddenly fit together in his mind. These were his old bags. There was the hole in them where Violet shot at the bandits as they rode away with what he thought was his gold. Damian's rank aroma wafted up from them, and he heard the laughter again as surely as if it was right there on the porch with him.

A groan that turned into a howl erupted from his chest. He left the bags on the porch as he ran through the living room and into the bedroom where he jerked on his trousers and a shirt. He buttoned the shirt as he hurried toward the barn and saddled Coaly, Missy right at his heels. He had a foot in the stirrup before he realized he was barefoot, but he didn't take time to go back into the house for his boots.

Thousands of horrible visions ran through his mind as he rode, hell-bent for leather, toward Dodsworth. Damian and all three of the others had just bought themselves an appointment with a noose and the nearest oak tree if they'd harmed a single hair on Violet's head. He'd actually thought those devils would return right after they found the gold wasn't in the saddlebags, but when they didn't he just figured they had cut their losses and gone on to Mexico like they'd said. He'd been a complete fool to let himself believe that.

She was dead. The pain in his heart wouldn't pulsate like it did if she was alive. Tears stung his eyes and flowed down his cheeks, the morning breeze cooling them as they dripped onto the front of his shirt. He'd track them down one at a time and make them wish they'd never seen his face. He might be old and gray by the time he found them but it wouldn't matter. Not anymore. Without Violet he was

only half a man anyway. So why farm the land he'd
bought? Why live? After the revenge he'd simply lay down
and die. Maybe she'd be waiting for him on the other side
of the white tunnel this time.

A crowd of townspeople watched the raging inferno
when he pulled back the reins and Coaly came to a halt in
front of the house. "Violet?" he screamed, all the pent up
rage, love, and fright a woeful wail as fears became reality.
There was no way she could have gotten out of that, not if
she wasn't already in the crowd. And if she was, she would
have already been on her way to let him know she was
alive.

"She's not out here," Maggie Listen drew her wrapper
around her body and shivered. "We smelled the smoke and
came out to see what it was. By the time we got here it
was already too big to put out. I'm sorry, Orrin."

"Are you sure she's not somewhere? Have you searched
the whole place?" He grasped at straws.

"We yelled and yelled for her. She's just not out here.
We can't get in close enough to see anything. It's so hot
and so big," she said, shaking her head.

Helplessly, he stood there and watched the house and
stable collapse into nothing more than a heap of memories.
The strange sweet sounds of music filled the air for just a
split second when a ceiling beam hit the piano keys. Was
it a sign that Gabriel had called Violet home at that very
moment? He bowed his head and a fresh batch of tears
streamed down his face, as Orrin Wilde began to mourn.

Maggie was wise enough to step away from the man and
give him his moment of grief. Next week she'd take him
a cobbler or something and listen to him talk about his
sweet Violet. Maggie could have easily fallen in love with
Orrin Wilde. Lord, but that man could dance even better
than she could, and she'd always held onto the idea that
someday a man would fall from Heaven just for her. But
she wouldn't ever have Orrin now. Violet could have had

him if she'd lived. Now he'd never be fit for any woman. Violet would haunt him the rest of his life.

Dawn was born as the blazes devoured the last of the house. When its furious appetite was sated, it simply died, leaving a pile of gray ash and glowing embers in its wake. Orrin sat on the ground in front of his horse. His mind refused to accept what his eyes saw. His Violet was among those ashes. She was no more than the piano or the floor boards. The bedstead stood like a sentinel amongst the ashes of where her bedroom used to be. Was that where she'd been when the fire started? Had her bed been a funeral pier?

He noticed that the kitchen stove was still in place where the kitchen had been. Maybe she'd been at the stove when the fire started. Or had that Damian tied her to a kitchen chair and made her watch as he started the fire? The thought made Orrin shudder from his scalp all the way to his bare feet. Several people stopped by to say a few comforting words as they went back to their own homes. No one knew about the saddlebags; few knew about the bandits and the night Violet had stood them off single-handed. They just thought a freak accident had occurred and took their friend and neighbor with it.

"Orrin?" Jed's hand clamped onto the man's shoulder. "We smelled smoke when we woke up and when I went to the cabin I found the saddlebags on the porch. Is this what it looks like?"

"Damian and those men did this to get back at me for the way Violet humiliated them. He threw the saddlebags on the porch and then laughed as he rode away," Orrin whispered hoarsely.

"Did they find her?" Jed asked, knowing the answer before he even asked.

"No. Maggie said they called and called but she didn't answer." Orrin's voice broke and he looked up toward the cloudless blue sky.

"Let's go home. I brought the wagon. Didn't know what we might need. Tie your horse on behind. Emma is going to go to pieces." Jed didn't even try to cover the pain in his voice.

"All right," Orrin said. Tomorrow he would deed his land to Jed and begin the journey. When it ended, he would be ready to go on to eternity. They couldn't be together in this lifetime, but surely God wouldn't stand in their way for eternity.

Missy threw back her head and set up a howl and somewhere another dog joined her. Even the animals knew a tragedy had occurred. "Come on girl, let's go home. We've got a lot to do," Orrin picked the pup up and put her in the back of the wagon.

He'd no more than set her down when she threw back her head and let out with another mournful howl which was answered by either an echo or another dog. She jumped down and took off in a run toward the house. "Come back, Missy," Orrin commanded but she simply howled again.

Orrin ran after her, careful to stay away from the burned places on the lawn that were still hot. "You crazy mutt, get back here," he yelled. But she kept running and running, stopping only long enough to howl and get her answer back on the wind.

Jed tossed the reins down in the wagon and joined Orrin in the chase. Whatever could that silly dog be chasing after at a time like this anyway? Then Jed recognized the howl on the other side of the house. It was Katy. She howled just like her mother, Ginger. The dog had found safety after all and that's what Missy was going for. Her sister was calling to her and she wasn't going back to the farm without her.

"It's Katy," Jed called out to Orrin. "I'd know that mournful howl anywhere. Sounds just like Ginger when she's got a coon in the tree. Missy is going to her. Be careful of those hot spots. Why didn't you wear your boots?"

"Didn't know I didn't have them on until I was mounting Coaly. Didn't take time to go get them," he said between breaths as he followed the dog's yips.

"There is Katy by the pond," Jed said excitedly. "Look at Missy licking her face. Violet must not have had her in the house after all. She told Emma last week the pup had been sleeping on the rug beside her bed but she wasn't about to admit that to you."

"Come on Katy. Come on Missy," Orrin called to the dogs who ran to his open arms. He buried his face in the smoky fur of Violet's dog and sobbed.

"It's all right, man. Let's go home now. We'll take her back with Missy and she'll be fine," Jed slung his arm around Orrin's shoulder.

Katy wiggled away from Orrin and ran back to the pond, Missy right on her trail. She stopped and waited. The man was here now, but why didn't he follow her?

"Come on you silly dogs," Jed coaxed them, but they didn't move.

Katy threw back her head and moaned.

"I'll go get her. She's probably afraid to go back toward the house," Orrin said.

He reached down to pick the puppy up and saw a piece of burned material floating just beyond his reach. His forehead furrowed in wonder and he pushed the brush away from the edge of the pond to see a pair of blackened legs stuck down in the water.

"Violet?" He screamed and tore at the reeds between him and the body. By the time he reached her, Jed was right behind him, wading the water in his boots.

"My Lord, she made it out of the house," Jed mumbled. "Is she alive, Orrin? Check her pulse. Is she breathing?"

"Just barely," Orrin answered as he picked her up and held her close to his chest. "Don't die, Violet," he whispered into the dark wet hair as he kissed her ashen face over and over. "Please don't die. I love you so much."

Chapter Twelve

By the time Orrin laid Violet on the bed in the cabin, Emma was in the room. She took one look at her best friend and commenced issuing orders. "Orrin, you go fill two basins. One with cold water and one with warm. And there will be a ball of rolled bandage in the basket beside the sink. Bring the whole basket. I'll need the rest of the emergency things in there, too. Sarah, you take Lalie Joy and sit on the porch in the swing with her. Mary, you and Jimmy fill up the wash tub in the back yard of our house and give those two puppies a bath. Molly, you be ready with a towel to dry them when they get the smoke all washed out of their fur. Jed," she whispered his name, only a bit of anguish coming through, "please comfort Orrin and don't let him back in here until I'm finished."

"Is she going to live?" Jed whispered back, holding Emma close and giving thanks for her at the same time.

"I don't know. Violet has a strong will and until I get her washed I won't know what's burn and what's smoke damage or dirt." Emma took the basket from Orrin's hand and shooed the whole bunch of them out the door.

Orrin shook his head. "I can't go."

"Yes, you can. Violet would shudder if she thought you'd stayed in the room with what I'm about to do. Kiss her and get out, Orrin. Right now." Emma left no room for argument.

Tears dripped down Orrin's face as he leaned forward to kissed Violet gently on her colorless lips. The tear drops settled on her face in minuscule puddles. Pure, unadulterated, liquid love. Somewhere in that land between the living and the dead, Violet felt a tug to return from the peaceful light she slowly traveled toward. She hesitated just a moment when the warmth of a healing power touched her face. She looked back, and when she looked forward again the light had dimmed. Restless, yet deep black sleep replaced the peace of the brilliant light.

"Okay, my friend," Emma said, "we're going to clean you up now." She used the scissors in the basket to cut down each sleeve of a stained, filthy nightgown. Then she cut it all the way down the front and peeled it away from Violet's body. "I'm starting at the bottom, Violet," Emma spoke softly in case her friend could hear her through the darkness of sleep and pain, "because that's where the worst of it looks to me."

Emma soaked the rags in cold water and began gently cleaning. The water in the basin turned black, but the burns were concentrated on her lower legs and feet, with the blisters on the bottom of her feet being the worst of the lot. She passed the basin out the door for new cold water five times before she finished the tedious job. Then she soaked Violet's hands in warm water, cleaned her broken, ragged fingernails, and washed her filthy hair.

"Jed, take Lalie Joy from Sarah and send her up to the house to get one of my nightgowns from the wardrobe. Tell her to bring a pair of drawers and a robe as well," she said through a crack in the door.

"Is she . . ." Orrin stopped pacing the living room floor long enough to look up.

"She's still sleeping and that's good, Orrin," Emma said. "I'll talk to you in a minute."

"Should I go for the doctor?" Jed asked.

"Not yet. Burns are bad, but I think she's all right other than those," Emma said.

"They didn't . . ." Orrin left the sentence hanging in the air.

"Just burns, Orrin," Emma said, staring him right in the eye.

While she waited for Sarah to return with the clothing, Emma applied ointment to the blisters on the bottom of Violet's feet and bandaged them loosely. The other burns were bright red, so she doctored them but didn't cover them with bandages. "It'll be a while before you walk again and even longer before you jump out there on the dance floor with Orrin Wilde. You better get well, though. Maggie sure likes the way he can dance. Never know, she might step right in and take him away from you, lady."

Violet heard something calling to her in the depths of the blackness. An urgency for her to go back—and she didn't know the way. Ahead the light had faded into nothing, and behind her was total darkness. Her feet, which had been floating toward the light, were suddenly on the ground and they hurt. She took one step, gently, easily. It was painful; but a tiny pinpoint of light showed somewhere down the trail. Something warm puddled up on her cheek again, and it eased the tremendous pain in her feet as she took one more small step. She heard voices somewhere toward the light. Emma. Jed. The children all talking at once. Lalie Joy whimpering and Emma comforting her. Then it was too quiet. She took another small step, and Orrin's presence filled the beam of light. He whispered something in her ear, but she couldn't make out the words, just the tone and the need to keep going.

"How bad are the burns?" Orrin asked Emma.

"Her feet are really serious. Blisters across the whole bottoms. The tops are red but no blisters. A few on her legs just above the ankles. Again, red but no blisters. If we can keep the infection out of her feet, she'll be all right, Orrin. It'll take a while before she can walk. I'll come down tonight with a pin and drain those blisters. Can't do it until after the sun goes down and the moon comes up or they'll infect for sure. Then we'll keep them clean and change the bandages every day. The ointment has a drawing power. Way I see it, she ran through the fire. The blazes caught the tail of her gown as she fled and burned her legs. She must have dropped and rolled in the grass from the stains on her gown, then crawled to the water. Her fingernails were a torn mess so her fingers might be a little sore for a few days. And I don't know if you noticed it or not but there was a rope around one wrist. At least the remnants of one. I'd say whoever set fire to her house tied her and she managed to break loose."

"I'm going to kill those four," Orrin said.

"Why? So you can hang for murder? That won't heal Violet one whit faster, and it'll break her heart. I won't listen to you talk like that, Orrin." Emma pointed her finger at his nose. "It's bad enough that she's had to endure this kind of thing. She's going to be devastated about losing her home, but losing you would be the end."

"I don't know about that," Orrin said, dropping his head into his hands.

"Trust me." Emma touched his shoulder. "And remember that old verse in the Good Book that says something about vengeance belonging to the Lord. He'll take care of those men and somehow, someday, you'll find out about it. Violet is going to need you for the next several weeks.

I could move her up to our house to take care of her but I think she'll heal faster if you are here with her."

"I don't know about that, either. Seems that all we do is aggravate each other. But I'm glad you're willing to leave her here, Emma. I want to be here for her." Orrin nodded. "I'll make a pallet and sleep beside her bed until she wakes."

"Then we're all going home and make breakfast. I'll send one of the kids down with some food in a little while. Don't know when Violet will wake up or if she'll be able to eat when she does, but you need to keep eating so you'll have the strength to take care of her," Emma said. "Now let's go, kids. Violet needs quiet so she can heal."

Orrin pulled up a chair and sat beside the bed. Violet lay so still, breathed so shallowly, that he wondered if each breath would be her last. Her face was still as pale as the white gown covering her body. Long dark lashes hid those haunting gray eyes that had mesmerized him as a child and invaded his dreams all the years he was working the mine in California. Emma had braided her dark hair into a single plait and it hung over her left shoulder all the way to her waist. One errant strand had already made its way out of the braid and Orrin brushed it away from her forehead. How could he have ever left this woman for an adventure? Talk about the impetuosity and stupidity of youth. They could have been old married people with four or five kids by this time. He'd ruined it all with his dreams. When she awoke she'd blame him for the whole ordeal, and rightly so. If he'd stayed home in Blue Ridge where he belonged, those bandits wouldn't have been after his gold or burned down her home.

Violet stopped in her journey to rest for a little while. Every step was pure torture on her feet. Someone ministered to her poor body, and somewhere in the recesses of her subconscious, she knew she was clean and sleeping soundly. Suddenly, an angel touched her forehead. Just a brush of gentleness and a soft whisper from someone who cared about her. Could it be Orrin? Was he really the one who kept beckoning her back to the real world and away from the peacefulness of eternity? No, Orrin ran away to the gold mines. He didn't care that he'd broken her heart. She found a spot of green grass and sat down to think. Did she want to go back? The floating sensation with no pain was so much more wonderful than walking on her hurting bare feet. Somehow she knew that if she chose to wake up, the choice wouldn't be hers to float toward the light any more.

Orrin picked up her hand and kissed each fingertip encrusted with bloody scabs where she had pulled herself along at the expense of tearing her nails into the quick. Sarah brought a platter with breakfast food on it. Scrambled eggs, biscuits, a slab of cured ham fried crisp. None of it looked good to Orrin but he thanked the child and made himself eat a few bites. When he finished, he set the dish on the table in the kitchen/living room combination of the cabin. He returned to his vigil, letting his eyes start at the top of Violet's dark hair and travel down to the white bandages covering her feet. Emotional exhaustion made him nod off and practically fall off the chair after a few minutes. He couldn't make himself lay on the floor beside the bed, but he had to sleep, so he rounded the bed and stretched out beside her. He picked up her hand and held it loosely. If she moved even a bit, he'd awaken. He shut his eyes and dozed fitfully.

Violet had made her decision. She was tired of walking on sore feet. She turned and looked back and the light was there again. A bright, beckoning light that said she could float again if she only stood up and kept her eyes straight forward. She didn't have to take another step. Never had to hurt. She longed for the peace. Wanted it so badly. Then a vine wrapped itself around her hand just like it had done in the dream she'd had before that evil man appeared. She couldn't go back as long as the vine held her tightly. She struggled against it but it just got tighter. Something told her that she'd have to go the other way to untangle the hold before she could find the eternal peace her soul craved.

She opened her eyes. Puppies barked in the distance. Children's giggles joined the yipping. A cricket sang a sorrowful tale of woe somewhere off in a corner not far away. She was stretched out on her back on a strange bed and she was awake, but the vine in her dreams still held her hand tightly, making her fingers ache. Her feet burned like they were on fire. A sudden vision of running through flames materialized on the ceiling above her. Confusion filled her breast. She could smell the smoke and hear Katy whining. She had to get them out of the fire, but she was tied to the bed. She struggled against the rope but she couldn't make it break.

Orrin awoke with a start to find Violet pulling her hand away from his. Her eyes were fixed on the ceiling and were wide with fear. She was panting like she'd run a mile and she yanked at her hand. He let go and she sat straight up, drew her feet up, winced at the pain and tried to stand on the bed.

"No, Violet, you can't put weight on your feet, honey. Lay back down. Don't even try to stand up. It's all right. I'm here," Orrin said.

"There's flames, Orrin. I have to shoot the rope and untie Katy. We're going to burn up if I don't. I have to walk through the flames," she said, staring ahead as if in a trance. "Please Orrin, don't let Katy die. Help her. Untie that rope. I can shoot mine off. He gave me a gun. Just one bullet to shoot myself with." She raised her hand and held the imaginary pistol in the palm.

"It's all over. You're alive. Your feet are blistered. That's why they burn. Lay back down, honey. I'll be right here."

"No you won't. You're going to run away to California

and leave me standing at the altar. You won't be here when I wake up. Did you know that Zeb died? I married him and he died," she whispered. She fell back on the bed and shut her eyes but her breathing was less shallow.

Orrin wept. Her mind was affected. She was a strong, independent woman but not strong enough to overcome that kind of experience. Not many women could. Tears bathed his cheeks and dripped again onto her face as he studied her expression. A frown cut furrows into her forehead. What could she be seeing behind those closed eyes? He wondered. That villain had tied her to the bed and left a gun with one bullet. One bullet to shoot herself, and she'd shot the rope.

Violet didn't want the rain drops from Heaven to drip on her face. That meant the angels weren't going to let her through to the peace. They were giving her a consolation prize and she wanted more. Agitation filled her as she opened her eyes again. What on earth was she doing in bed with Orrin Wilde? Mercy, he'd run off years ago, back before she married Zeb McDonald. Zeb would come home any minute and there'd be the devil to pay if he caught Orrin Wilde stretched out in the bed beside her. She turned her eyes without moving her head. There was a wash stand. But her pitcher and bowl set had blue flowers. The one in the corner of the bedroom where she was lying was pure white. And the bedstead was wooden. Hers was made of iron . . . hot iron. It almost burned her fingers when she untied Katy and crawled to the water.

Zeb is dead, a voice in the back of her mind reminded her bluntly. *Your house burned down and you barely escaped. Your feet are burning because you ran through fire and jumped through the window to escape.*

"Katy?" she screamed and bolted straight up again.

"She's fine, Violet." Orrin wrapped his arms around her and held her close.

"She didn't die in the fire? I got her out all right?" She squirmed out of his embrace. "Don't you lie to me, Orrin."

"She's fine. I'll go get her if you want me to." He could hardly believe his ears. Her eyes were bright and alive and her voice was strong.

"Yes, I want to see her. I don't believe you," Violet said bluntly.

Orrin eased off the bed, careful not to touch her feet. He padded across the living room floor and opened the front door. Katy and Missy both slept on the front porch, tangled up together. He picked up both pups and carried them back to the bedroom. "Jimmy and Mary gave them a bath to get the smoke off," he said, putting Katy in her outstretched arms.

"My poor, poor baby." Violet buried her face into the puppy's silky, clean fur. "We really are alive, aren't we, Orrin? But oh, no, my house is burned down. It's all gone. I have nothing. Did they save my sewing machine?"

"Nothing was saved," Orrin said.

The enormity of what he said hit her like the engine of a train going full blast down the tracks. Her nerves exploded and her soul split like a broken glass window when a child's ball hit it. A sob caught somewhere in her chest and tore from her mouth in a ragged wail.

"Don't worry, Violet. It's all material. It can all be replaced. The important thing is that you are alive. That your mind is whole after an ordeal like that." Orrin put his arm around her but she shrugged it away.

"Don't touch me, Orrin Wilde. Go away and let me alone," she said.

"All right," Orrin said, his mouth set firmly. If that's the way she wanted it then that's the way she could have it. He didn't have to sit right beside her. He had work to do. Things that needed his attention other than shedding tears over a woman who didn't want him in the room. She certainly didn't need him or for that matter want him. And he couldn't really blame her. After all, it was his fault that she'd just lost everything she had and held dear. He left the door to the bedroom open and listened to her weep as he pulled on his boots and took Missy out the front door.

He sat on the porch for a while, wondering if he should leave her totally and go on about his business or what. He didn't even hear Jed, but suddenly there was his friend sitting on the front porch, whittling on a twig.

"She wake up yet?" Jed finally asked.

"Yes, and told me to get out. Can't say as how I blame her. If it hadn't been for me, the man wouldn't have had that grudge." Orrin looked up at the cloudless, blue summer sky. He wouldn't cry in front of Jed again.

"She'll get over it," Jed said. "She'll just have to work through it in her mind. That's all. She eat anything yet? Emma says she's got to eat to keep her body strong so she don't get fever or infection."

"Then she'll eat," Orrin said with a set to his jaw that almost made Jed bite his lip to keep from laughing. Give them something to fight about and they'd make it fine. They belonged together. That was as plain as the fact the sun came up every morning. But they'd have to work through their fears before they realized what every one else in Dodsworth already knew.

Orrin's step was determined as he opened the door. He squared his shoulders and picked up the platter of cold breakfast. If he had to shove every bite into her mouth, he was up to the task. Emma said she had to eat and making her eat was something he could very well do.

Violet could have bitten the end right off her tongue for saying such caustic words to Orrin. But blast his good-looking face all to the devil anyway. What gave him the right to lay on the bed right next to her and her in nothing more than a nightgown. She recognized the house she was in when he left. They'd taken her to Emma and Jed's cabin. The place where Emma and Jed first lived when they married. To the very bedroom they'd shared for months before they were really committed to being a married couple. Violet wondered if the bedroom would work the same magic on her and Orrin. She doubted it. Not now. Who'd want a woman who would probably limp for the rest of her life? Who could never chase children or play with the dogs out in the yard. No man needed a woman to hang around his neck like an albatross. Nothing more than a burden upon him. Even if he wanted to court her before, he sure wouldn't want to now. He just felt guilty because it was his fault that the man came back and burned her house.

She heard Jed's voice but she couldn't hear the conversation. Didn't even want to hear it. The realization that she couldn't even run the treadle sewing machine and make a living hit home about then and her anger doubled. "What are you doing?" she demanded when Orrin carried the platter of food to the bedside.

"You are going to eat. Emma says if you don't you'll get fever and infection. So you will eat, Violet Daniels," he said.

"I'll do what I want and nothing more," she snapped.

"Then you better want to eat." His voice rose an octave and challenged her.

Violet's stomach growled. Katy wagged her tail and sniffed at the aroma of the food. Orrin's eyes flashed and Violet almost laughed. Nothing was funny. Not the hurt in her legs and feet. Not the fact that her house was gone, along with all her memories for the past years. She remembered the night she held off the bandits with her .22 rifle and later sat on the settee and laughed until tears rolled down her cheeks. The way she felt right then wasn't totally unlike that. Either laugh or cry. Either eat or go hungry just to win the argument.

"Well?" Orrin asked.

"I can't very well eat if you don't give me the plate, now can I? You'd just stand there with all that good food and let me starve, I suppose. Well, that's what I'd expect of you, Orrin Wilde. Now give me that plate and put Katy on the floor. What I don't eat, she's going to want," Violet said.

"I'll feed you," he said, sitting down beside her.

"I don't use my feet to put food in my mouth," she smarted off to him. "I'll feed myself, Orrin. While I do it I'll tell you about the fire. There's nothing wrong with my mind. I'm completely saddened by the loss of all my things, but I will survive. I've survived lots of difficulties in my life, so I'll make it through this, too. Soon as I'm able to get around I'll get that mess cleaned up and then I'll rebuild my house."

Not if I have anything to do with it, he thought as he handed her the plate and picked up Katy. *The only way you'll leave this house is to move in with me in the house I'm building for you, Violet. We'll overcome this as well as the past.*

Chapter Thirteen

A hot breeze blew across the porch where Violet sat
sideways on the swing with her bandaged feet propped up
on a pillow. Orrin had gone to oversee something about
the house he was building on the land she'd sold him a
few weeks ago. Emma was sewing, and Mary had brought
a stack of garments to Violet to finish the handwork on.
Violet's fingernails had grown out enough in the past six
days so that they weren't sore any more. The ointment
Emma used sure did the trick. Too bad her feet weren't
healing as fast.

She picked up a blue and white gingham checked dress
and measured a three-inch hem. At that, the way Mary was
growing, the dress probably wouldn't make it through the
whole school year. "I bet if you went back up to the house
and brought me Emma's crochet thread and a hook, I could
fancy this up with a little lace around the collar and down
the front of the button placket," Violet said.

"Then I'll have the prettiest dress of any of the girls on

139

the first day of school." Mary's blue eyes lit up. "Momma said I'm supposed to stay with you case you need something from in the house though."

"Tell you what." Violet smiled and it actually reached her light gray eyes. "You go in there and bring me a glass of water. We'll sit it right here and I'll be fine while you run up to the big house and back. I bet you won't be gone more than ten minutes. Tell Emma I sent you because I've got the hem done and I need something else to keep me busy."

She shaded her eyes from the sun and watched Mary's faded pink dress whip against her legs as she ran toward the two-story house just up the hill from the cabin. Mary ran like a feisty colt, all long arms and gangly legs going every which way. It wouldn't be long though until she and Sarah both were young ladies. The thunder of hooves caused Violet to turn her head sharply. There was too much noise for it to be Orrin coming home. He rode out on one horse. She could swear there were at least four horses coming.

Four.

A cold chill started at the base of her spine and raced to her scalp, making it prickle with fear. Damian had returned to finish the job. She couldn't stand on her feet to run away or to even get in the house for protection. Her eyes darted from the swing to the door. Could she hop on her heels? They were the least burned. Emma said she'd probably instinctively ran on the balls of her feet, protecting as much of her tender bare feet as possible.

She swung her feet out onto the floor and had her hand on the arm of the swing when she heard the war whoops and all the pent up fright escaped with a whoosh as she exhaled loudly. Four horses thundered from behind the big house and John Whitebear let out another whoop as he reached down and gathered Molly up onto his horse. It was a game they'd played ever since John Whitebear had befriended Jed. Violet pulled her legs back up to the swing and eased them down on the pillow.

The Indians brought their ponies to an abrupt halt right in front of the cabin, and John Whitebear set Molly down. "I have just heard about the loss of your home and your burned feet," he said, looking into Violet's eyes.

"Will you take me back to the house after a while real fast so my braids fly out behind my head?" Molly asked, breathlessly.

"Of course I will." John Whitebear nodded. "But first we have to see about Violet's burns."

"They're healing," Violet said.

"And they will heal faster." John Whitebear opened his saddlebags and brought out several fleshy leaves of a plant. "I found a woman in Guthrie with this growing in her garden. I begged for the leaves and for a starting of the plant for you and Emma. She must have thought I was going to scalp her because she said I could have all I wanted and she disappeared into her cabin so fast I wondered if she'd ever been there. It will heal your feet quicker than anything. Now let's unwrap all that bandage and see what we can do."

"Are you sure about this, John?" Violet asked.

"It is what my wife uses when we burn ourselves. It has healing power. Now, raise up those skirts and let's see," he said, taking his knife from a scabbard on the side of his pants.

Orrin was pleased with the progress on the house. It was similar to Emma and Jed's place. He just hoped Violet was sincere when she said she loved the spaciousness of their home. He'd given the carpenters a few more pointers and was on his way back to the cabin when he heard the thunder of hooves. His first thought was the same as Violet's. The bandits were returning to finish the job of killing Violet. Fear gripped his heart in a tight vice when he remembered that Mary was going to sit on the porch with her while he was gone. They'd harm the child as well as Violet. The horses continued to come closer to the house and then he heard the whoops and hollers of a bunch of drunk bandits, followed by Molly's squeals. Every hair on his arms and neck stood straight up. He whipped out the .22 rifle from the sheath on the side of Coaly's saddle and hit the back door of the cabin in a run.

By the time he reached the front door he heard a voice say something about lifting her skirts and he put his finger on the trigger. Vengeance might belong to the Lord as Violet said. But Damian was a dead man walking and didn't even know it right at that moment. He covered the distance from the back door to the front porch in only a few quick strides and had the rifle on his shoulder when he kicked the door open.

"Get back," he growled.

"Oh, Orrin, come and meet John Whitebear and his friends." Violet looked up innocently. "Good grief, put that gun down. John brought something his wife uses to heal burns."

Orrin didn't know whether to shoot the man or drop down on his knees and give up thanks. Bewilderment and confusion filled his breast. "I heard riders and Molly screaming and I thought . . ." He lowered the gun.

"You thought it was the bandits. So did I," Violet said. "It's a game Molly plays with John Whitebear. He yells war whoops and she runs out in the yard with her arms up. He picks her up and swings her beside him. They've played it ever since the land run. Put the gun down, Orrin. John is going to try something on my feet. He says it will heal them faster."

Orrin didn't know if he wanted them to heal any faster. As it was, he was having trouble thinking about the day when Violet would leave the cabin. She'd already begun to talk about the way her new house would be built and to look at the catalogs for a new sewing machine.

"I can understand your fear," John Whitebear said. He stuck out his hand to shake with the white man. It was evident he was in love with Violet from the way his eyes softened when he looked at her. That was good. Violet needed someone to love her. She was a good, strong woman. One John's wife admired. But his wife had mentioned several times that Violet needed children.

Orrin shook hands with the man and sat down on the edge of the porch. "Sorry about that," he said.

"Don't be. You're just protecting your woman," John said.

Violet felt high color filling her cheeks. Orrin cleared his throat and turned his head quickly to look at Molly, who was telling one of the other Indians about her new sister, Lalie Joy. John Whitebear smiled brightly, showing off beautiful white teeth. He had been right.

"We will take all the bandages off first," he explained as he unwound the white cloth. "You did burn them badly. Had I known before now we could have shortened the time of healing. If you had put the plant on them in the first hours you would be walking today. Now this will feel slick and cool. It will draw the fire and pain out. Once a day for a week and you will be up and walking. Maybe a little slow at first." He used his knife to split the long, fleshy leaves lengthwise and lay them gently on her feet. After he'd applied just enough bandage to hold the leaves in place, he split another one and used it as a swab to smear the slick liquid from the inside on the burns on her ankles and lower legs.

"That feels wonderful," Violet said, smiling. Orrin's heart twisted up in a lonely knot. Not once had she smiled at him like that. Not since they were kids in Blue Ridge. One week, the Indian said. It wasn't long enough. He needed a month or more to convince her of his love.

"What is it?" Orrin asked.

"I don't know what you white people call it. We simply refer to it as fire plant. It grows easily and works well. I brought a piece with roots. If you put it in a pot in your kitchen window it will grow and be ready for the next accident. One leaf can be split several times. I think this plant will last through the week, and then the plant can grow new ones for the next time," John Whitebear explained.

"Thank you," Orrin said, not knowing if he meant it or not.

"You are very welcome. I'm glad Violet has a man now to make sure no one hurts her," John Whitebear said. "Tell me about the evil man who did this. I heard it was a bandit who failed to rob you and came back for revenge."

"That's exactly what happened," Violet said. "But I managed to get away and to crawl to the pond to cool my feet. Orrin found me and brought me here."

"Good. Now you put this on the kitchen window. It doesn't require water so often. My wife says you can kill it if you water too much. Only when it is very dry. The leaves hold the water like cactus. No more ointment. Just these leaves and in one week you will be walking. Oh, and use these until your feet are ready to be shoved down into the white woman's boots." He handed her a pair of soft deerskin moccasins from his saddlebags.

"Can she dance?" Molly asked. "Orrin danced with her and me and Mary said they was in love. Sarah said it wasn't so, but me and Mary could tell."

John Whitebear threw back his head and roared. His friends did the same. "At that, I will take Molly back to her own yard. You wait right here, my pretty child, and we will ride a little ways down the road and come back. When you hear the whoops, put your arms up for me. I'll hope our paths cross again, Orrin Wilde. Take care of Violet."

Orrin watched in amazement as John Whitebear and his friends rode away and then turned abruptly and let out a series of bone-chilling whoops. They raced toward Molly, who didn't budge. Orrin had to fight every ounce of his better judgment as they rode straight at Molly. With a graceful sweep John gathered Molly up onto the horse and sped back to the big house.

"It's a show, isn't it?" Violet smiled, and Orrin's heart melted into a puddle somewhere in the middle of his chest.

"My heart is still pounding," he said.

"Well, how's the house coming along?" She changed the subject.

"Just fine. It'll be done before the cold weather. I need to start clearing land and getting wood stacked up for winter," he said.

"And I'm holding you back. I told you, just put me up at Emma's. She can keep an eye on me and boss me around," Violet said.

"No," Orrin said. "Are you ready to go inside? If you can sit at the end of the table and make biscuits like you did yesterday, I'll fry a rabbit and some potatoes. I shot one on the way back. It's hanging on my saddle horn."

"I can do that." Violet held up her arms. Orrin scooped her up and she felt small in his embrace. Looking back in honest reflection she'd never felt like a giant, gangly woman when she was with Orrin. "Does that hurt your back?" she asked.

"Hardly even know it's been hurt anymore. You did a fine job of taking care of me, Violet," he said, opening the front door with the toe of his boot. "Where is Mary? I thought she was staying with you."

"I sent her home to get a crochet hook and some thread," Violet said. "Thank goodness she wasn't here. If that had been Damian and the rest of his friends, she would have been in danger."

"Violet, I think I should go take care of that. We can't live in fear the rest of our lives. I could bring him in to the sheriff and the law could do the rest. I wouldn't have to kill the man," Orrin said.

She slowly shook her head. To send Orrin off like that would be tempting fate too closely. She couldn't do it, not even if she had to worry every day for the rest of her life. She could not send the man she loved above all others into a dangerous situation.

Loved? Beyond all others?

"No, please don't, Orrin," she whispered, barely getting the words out before the sound of a buggy stopped at the front of the cabin and Maggie's "Hello" floated across the front porch.

Orrin's brown eyes locked with Violet's gray ones. He saw everything he wanted in a wife and the mother of his future children hiding down in the depths of her soul. She saw a good man, one who'd disappointed her but who'd redeemed himself since. One who'd make a good husband and father. The instant came and was gone in the blinking of an eye and before either of them could speak, Maggie was in the room, carrying a basket over her arm.

"Hi," she said cheerfully. "I hope you haven't started dinner. I brought it with me. Got a fried chicken and baked sweet potatoes. Momma sent a loaf of fresh bread, still warm from the oven. We were waiting on it or I'd a been here sooner. Now you go get washed up, Orrin, and I'll set the table. I passed John Whitebear on the road. Said he put some kind of Indian magic on your feet." She rattled as she found plates and cups to set the table.

"Momma said to say she was sorry but she had trouble finding the right hook," Mary said as she rushed in the front door. "John Whitebear stopped and talked about some kind of stuff he put on your feet. Momma said she'd heard of that kind of plant down in Georgia. Is it helping? Oh, Momma said I was to come on back home for lunch and let you and Orrin have a peaceful minute by yourselves." Mary came through the door talking. "Oh, hi, Maggie.

Guess they won't have some time all by themselves to fall in love if you are here. But I got to go. Momma says Sarah has to let me play with Lalie Joy while she makes biscuits for Daddy Jed."

Maggie giggled when Mary took off out the door in another one of her awkward runs. "Kids. Never know what they're going to say. Is the stuff John put on helping?" She deftly changed the subject. She might have a reputation for being scatterbrained but she wasn't stupid, and Orrin and Violet were both blushing as well as avoiding each other's eyes.

"Yes, he did, and it feels much better," Violet said. "Thank you for this nice gesture, Maggie. The smell of that bread is making my stomach growl."

"Well, Momma can make good bread," Maggie laughed. "If she could dance as well as she can make bread, I'd have some competition. By the way, I came prepared to stay the whole afternoon. That way, Orrin can get on with his business. Momma said she'd send one of the other girls for a day next week if you still need help. We just feel so bad about your house, Violet. Menfolks in town say they'll all pitch in and help rebuild when you get ready. They've already started cleaning up the mess. Wasn't one thing left to save. Preacher Elgin tried to work on the stove, but it was too far gone."

"Thank you, Maggie. And tell everyone else thanks. I'm beholden to all of you. Now, Orrin, if you're ready, let's eat this good food while it's still hot. Maybe you could bring in the rabbit after lunch and I'll help Maggie make a good soup for our supper," Violet said, her eyes brimming with tears at the thought of so much kindness.

Orrin ate but tasted nothing. One week and her feet would be healed if the magic worked. People in town were already cleaning up and getting ready to rebuild for her. He'd courted her once in Blue Ridge, but he was at loggerhorns with himself about how to go about doing it again.

They'd lived under the same roof, eating every meal together for the better part of a week. He could hear her soft breathing when she slept in the only bedroom and he crawled up the ladder to his bed in the loft. Before that he'd spent weeks in her house, being cared for by her soft hands and sharp tongue.

But the time had come for serious courting, and even with all the Wilde blood in his veins, he was tongue tied, had two left feet, and was all thumbs when it came to telling her exactly how he felt. One week. Two at the most. He'd better be thinking about how to convince her of his love . . . but where did he start?

"Orrin? Did you hear me?" Maggie cocked her head off to one side.

"I'm sorry. I guess I was wool gathering," Orrin said.

Maggie smiled. It was pretty evident what he was wool gathering about, too. The way he stole looks at Violet made Maggie's heart float. If a man who danced as well as Orrin Wilde looked at her with that same look, she'd feel like she'd died and gone straight to Heaven.

"I was asking how your house is coming along. When I rode past it a while ago it looked pretty nigh to finished," she said.

"The outside walls are almost done. Then we'll divide the inside and put the plaster on the walls. All the finish stuff, you know. That should start in about two weeks." He bit into a piece of chicken. Two weeks until Violet would need to make the decisions about wallpaper and all those feminine things that would make it her house. His heart dropped down into his boots. He'd never convince her in that length of time that he loved her and wanted to marry her. "Well, Maggie, that was a wonderful lunch, and I thank you for it. If you are sure about spending the afternoon, I think I'll go on and start getting wood ready for the winter."

"I'm sure. I brought two dresses Momma sewed up for Violet. She'll have to do the handwork. She's better at it than us anyway. But we knew she'd be needin' some things of her own." Maggie blushed herself, thinking about the drawers and camisoles she'd brought to go along with the dresses. She'd never mention those things in front of Orrin. Just thinking about them in a man's presence about made her speechless.

"Well, thanks again. I'll clean that rabbit and bring him in before I go. Think you ladies could make rabbit and dumplings? Haven't had good dumplings since your momma made them in Blue Ridge." Orrin smiled at Violet.

If he thinks he can remember the good times and then run off and leave me again he's got rocks for brains and cow chips for intelligence, she thought. "I remember how she made them. Now you get on to your business and Maggie and I'll spend an afternoon catching up and sewing."

Orrin just nodded. The softness in her eyes wasn't there like it had been before Maggie arrived. For just a fleeting moment, he'd thought they'd crossed all the barriers, but the moment passed. He wondered if they'd ever find it again.

"That man is in love with you," Maggie declared after she'd cut the rabbit into pieces and put it on to boil.

"Anna Marie says he's just beholden to me for taking care of him," Violet picked up the dress for Mary and began to edge the collar in finely crocheted lace.

"Anna Marie is as stupid as she looks," Maggie snorted. "She's running around town fussing about you staying in this cabin with him. But folks who know you ain't listenin' to one bit of it."

"I figured there'd be talk," Violet said quietly. Her quiet life had surely been the subject of gossip since Orrin landed on her doorstep.

"If they're talkin' about you, they're lettin' me rest," Maggie said with a laugh. "If he wasn't so besotted with you, I'd try to rope him. He can sure dance and that's what I want in a husband."

"Maggie, why do you keep saying that?" Violet asked.

"What? That he's besotted with you? Well, that's plain as the nose on your face, Violet McDonald. The man is in love with you. Or the part about dancing? Well, that part is like this. I can cook and I can sew. I'm not as smart as some women when it comes to important matters with talking. But I love to dance and I'm good at it. I guess I'm looking for a man who's good at it, too, because I know if he can dance he'll be more than a . . ." she stammered, looking for the right words. "It's like this, Violet. I don't want to marry up with a man like Jim Parsons who can't have fun. Who can't laugh or find anything funny in a day's living. A man who loves to dance, well, he's learned to have a good time. I'll be a good wife someday, but I won't be tied down to a life where I can't laugh and have a good time at it."

And they call Maggie scatterbrained, Violet thought. She had things figured out better than most women. "Sounds fine to me," Violet said. "But about that business of Orrin being in love with me. I don't think so."

"Don't matter what you think. The man is and that's a fact. Now you want me to put these undergarments away in that bedroom for you?"

"Yes, thank you," Violet said. "And thanks to all of you for making them for me."

"No thanks necessary, but you are welcome. They'll fit you for a while until you come to your senses and marry Orrin. Then when you get in the family way, they'll be too little," Maggie said.

"Maggie!" Violet exclaimed.

Maggie just laughed. "Can't change what's before our eyes, Violet. That'd be like trying to change Anna Marie into someone sweet and nice or Jim Parsons into an exciting fellow. It just ain't possible. Stop fighting and get well. He dances real good."

Chapter Fourteen

Violet shuffled from one side of the bed to the other. The leaves John Whitebear left to put on her feet had really worked magic. She chose one of the dresses Maggie's mother had made for Sunday morning services and looked forward to seeing familiar faces again. The dress was a simple calico day dress. A pale yellow background strewn with cornflower blue forget-me-nots. They'd guessed her size fairly well. The waist was only an inch too big and that might be because she hadn't had much of an appetite since the fire. The hem line could have been an inch shorter, but then it would have been perfect if she'd been wearing her Sunday boots with a heel rather than the soft moccasins John Whitebear left for her.

She pulled her hair back into a bun at the nape of her neck and perched one of Emma's hats on her head. It was a plain straw with a yellow band and small blue flowers in the middle of the bow at the back. Emma had declared she was to have it when she saw the dress Maggie brought. It

did match the dress well, and Violet almost felt human
again when she was dressed and ready to go that morning.
She heard Orrin bringing the buggy around and the children
giggling and yelling at her to hurry as they drove past in
Jed and Emma's wagon.

"Well?" She looked up to see Orrin standing in the door
of the bedroom. "Don't you look beautiful this morning."
His eyes were soft and his mouth begged for a kiss. Violet
recognized the look but she wasn't having any of it right
before church. Besides, she wasn't so sure she could stop
with one kiss again like she'd done the other two times she
found herself in his arms.

"Thank you." She picked up her Bible and started across
the room toward him. Her feet were still tender but she was
making progress.

Suddenly, she found herself swept off her sore feet and
in Orrin's arms. His eyes were twinkling and a smile covered his handsome face. "We better hurry a little bit or
we'll sure enough have to sit on the front row again," he
explained as he carried her through the house and set her
gently in the buggy seat.

"Thank you, Orrin," she said softly without looking at
him. "For everything these past days."

"Remember what the old folks said in Blue Ridge. What
goes around comes around. You took care of me," he said.

"You're just paying debts, then?" She bristled.

"Don't you be starting a fight with me today, Violet."
He smiled at her. "Because it's too pretty of a day to be
fighting. We got church, then a social, and you aren't going
to make me mad."

"Want to bet?" she said.

They rode in silence for most of the way to the church.
He wondered how in the world he would ever get her to
marry him and if he could live the life of rapid ups and
downs with her. One thing for sure, he'd never be bored.
She'd make him toe the line from daylight to dark every

day. She wondered if she could ever lay aside the doubts and let her heart follow the natural course. She'd always loved Orrin Wilde so that wasn't the problem. Trusting him was. He'd redeemed himself a thousand times, but one little thread of self-protecting reservation still kept its teeth sunk into her spirit.

"This thing like the ones we had at home?" he finally asked when he set the brakes on the buggy at the edge of the church yard. "Lots of food and everyone visiting?"

"Exactly," she nodded. "Emma said she was bringing an extra quilt for us and plenty of food."

"Good. I missed those kinds of things," he said, reaching up and picking her up like she was no heavier than Molly.

"I can walk," she protested. For the past three weeks, Orrin had carried her into the church when she hadn't been able to put her feet on the ground, but today she could have shuffled in on her own steam. "Put me down at the back door and I'll walk up to our pew."

She'd referred to the front pew as their pew. Orrin wanted to shout. But he didn't even answer. He wouldn't put her down at the doors for all the gold in California. He wanted Jim Parsons and every other man in all of Logan County to know that he'd staked a claim and they'd better keep their covetous eyes away from the widow McDonald. He continued to the church, where he carried her down the aisle to the front pew. Past Emma and Jed who beamed at the sight just like they did every Sunday. Past Anna Marie who drew her eyebrows down in a frown just like she did every Sunday. Right up to the place where he and Violet always sat. Preacher Elgin took his place behind the pew when Orrin had her settled and she had her hat resituated.

"We can begin now that Violet and Orrin are here. Once again, I want to mention how glad we are that Violet is healing nicely," he said in a big booming voice that didn't sound like it could possibly come from a man so small. "She's met death head on and come out of it with pain but at least alive. We are grateful that her good friend, Orrin Wilde, found her and is nursing her back to health, like she did him back at the first of the summer. I am glad he got well before this happened. I don't think many men in this town could carry Violet McDonald into church," he said, chuckling.

Violet smiled up at him. For the first time in her life she wasn't insulted when someone mentioned her size, and besides he was dead to rights. Jed might be able to carry her. He'd picked Emma up before. But Violet was a bit bigger than Emma. Alford couldn't have picked up half her weight, and Jim Parsons couldn't even bring himself to speak to her, much less pick her up and tote her into the church house.

After services, it didn't take the womenfolks long to throw quilts under the trees for a Sunday afternoon social. Boys ignored the girls and began choosing sides for a baseball game. Girls gathered in groups to talk about boys. A few clouds skittered across the skies and covered the sun, giving them all a respite from the heat for a little while.

Emma helped get Violet comfortable and Lalie Joy in her lap before she began unpacking two baskets of food. "You'll never believe the news I got this week," Emma said. "My stepmother has a brother who's been out east for several years. He's a doctor but he's tired of the big city and wants to have a small practice in a little town. Goodness knows he doesn't even have to work. Eulalie's folks left plenty of money to them both, but anyway, he wrote me a letter, asking about Dodsworth."

"You can't be serious," Violet said.

"Yes I am. I wrote him right back and told him that Dodsworth is pretty small but we needed a doctor really bad. You know if you'd been burned worse than you were or if something worse had happened we would have had to go all the way to Guthrie for a doctor. And the night Lalie was born, I'm just glad there wasn't any problems, because

I'd begun to think me and Sarah were going to have to deliver her by ourselves by the time Jed got back with the doctor." Emma set out fried chicken, potato salad, beans, fresh bread, and ginger cakes for dessert. Jed carried a gallon jug of sweet tea from the wagon, and Orrin followed him with another jug. Jimmy stopped Orrin to ask about a stray dog following him around, and Violet watched from a distance. Orrin was good with kids, just like Emma said. Jed handed his jug to his wife. He brushed a kiss across her upturned mouth and settled down on the quilt beside Violet.

"Hello," Anna Marie stopped at the edge of the quilt. "I'm chasing after little Alford so we can eat our lunch over there." She nodded back toward the church where Preacher Elgin's family had set up afternoon camp. "Did you see him come by this way?"

"Yes," Violet nodded. "He's over there with that gang of little girls. They're taking turns holding him. Doesn't look like he likes any part of it, though."

"No, he doesn't like to be held," Anna Marie said curtly. "You still expecting that man to make a decent woman out of you? Well, you'll be waiting a long time, Violet," she snipped. "You're just a big ugly woman . . ."

"Anna Marie, that is enough," Jed said with enough edge to his voice that she stopped and stared at him angrily.

"It'll be enough when I say it's enough," she said, pointing her finger at Jed. "You don't have a lick of sense when it comes to women either."

"Like Jed said, that's enough," Emma stood up, towering above Anna Marie. "You better go claim your son or else sit beside your husband before your big mouth and little brain gets your chubby fanny in more trouble than it can crawl out of on one Sunday afternoon."

"Don't you threaten me, Emma Thomas," Anna Marie took a step backwards.

"I'm not threatening anyone, sweetheart. I'm stating

facts. You are entitled to your opinions but you'd do well to keep them to yourself," Emma said in a voice so low no one else could hear. "Now go get your son."

"He still won't marry her," Anna Marie tossed over her shoulder as she stormed off.

"Sorry about that," Emma said. "Why didn't you take care of that snippit?" She turned on Jed who threw up his hands in protest.

"That's why I married a rebel woman with a mind of her own. You did just fine all by yourself, honey. I didn't need to step in." He chuckled.

"It's just Anna Marie. Alford is a saint." Violet giggled with them. "Now tell me more about this doctor."

"What doctor?" Orrin handed Emma his jug of tea and sat down so close to Violet his arm touched hers. The sensation was almost more than he could bear, but he wanted more and more of it.

"Emma's dad is married to Eulalie. It's her brother who might move to Dodsworth. He's a doctor back east," Violet explained.

"We need a doctor," Orrin nodded. "Between me and Violet we could probably keep him in business."

"Well, it'll take a couple of months for him to get his affairs in order and we thought if your house was finished up by then, and we get Violet's place rebuilt, we might offer to let him live in the cabin. 'Course he'd want to set up some kind of office in town. I thought maybe that room above the post office might be all right. Or maybe Duncan could let him have a space at the back of his store," Jed said.

"The house should be done by then," Orrin said seriously. "To get a doctor for Dodsworth, I'd be willing to chip in enough money to build him a little office. He'd just need a couple of rooms."

"Bet we could get someone to donate a little chunk of land if you'll do that," Jed said excitedly. "I'll send him a telegram tomorrow and let him know we're working on something."

"What's his name?" Violet asked. "How old is he?"

"I think he's about thirty. Tall. Dark. Handsome, I guess. Don't you look at me like that, Jed Thomas. I'm just stating facts. Eulalie calls him Jackson but I think that's his middle name. He goes by Dr. Everett Dulanis. He's engaged to a girl in Georgia. Carolina Prescott. I expect he'll be bringing her here before long. She's quite a socialite. She'll turn Dodsworth into a fashion plate." Emma took the baby from Violet and motioned for the four older children to join them.

After lunch and one game of baseball with the boys, Orrin gathered Violet up in his arms without an explanation and told the Thomas family they'd be back in time for night church. "We're going for a ride. I've got something I want Violet to see," he said.

"I want to go," Molly stood up and brushed the crumbs from her Sunday frock.

"Not this time," Orrin said. "I'll take you for a ride next Sunday. Today I've got something special I want Violet to see."

"You going to take her to the bedroom and kiss her?" Molly asked.

"Molly!" Emma exclaimed.

"Never know," Orrin said, and winked conspiratorially at the little girl.

"Now what's this all about?" Violet asked when he got her comfortable in the buggy seat. "You could have asked me if I wanted to go for a ride instead of just carrying me away."

"I didn't want an argument." Orrin flicked the reins and the horses turned around and headed back toward Emma and Jed's place. They passed the cabin and then the big house and still he drove on. Violet wondered where he might be taking her and why, but she wasn't asking. The silence was comfortable. A fight might come about if they started to talk, and she didn't want to spoil the time.

In a few minutes they topped a small rise, and there was the house. A mansion by Oklahoma standards in that day. Snowy white with two stories and eight white pillars holding up the galleries on the top of the balconies opening out from the bedrooms located behind doors with real glass windows.

"Galleries?" She whispered the single word.

"It's hot in Oklahoma during the summertime. We'll need the air and if it gets too hot we can move the bed out on the gallery and sleep out there," he explained, pride in every word. "Out in California they said that a rich man might afford six pillars for his home. I figured eight might be a little much for Oklahoma, but I'm only intending to build one house in my lifetime, Violet. Just one. So I made it big enough to house all my dreams. It's not a slap in the face for the folks still struggling to make a little cabin on their homesteads. It's just what I've always wanted and what I designed all those years when I was robbing the land of her gold out west."

He set the hand brake and whistled as he rounded the buggy to gather her into his arms and carry her up to the porch. "It's not finished inside yet but I want you to see it."

"Put me down and let me walk in the doors. You should save the job of carrying a woman over the threshold for your bride, Orrin," she said, struggling against his arms.

He turned the fancy knob on one of the doors and pushed it open with the tip of his boot, but he didn't set Violet down. He carried her right across the threshold before he gently put her on her tender feet in the middle of what would be called the foyer. He tilted her chin back and kissed her. A deep kiss that glued her to the floor. She couldn't have took a step away from him if her very life had depended on it.

"Oh, my," she said. Would she always feel like that about Orrin Wilde? The magic had never left. Just got misplaced for several years while they both grew up and found out that they were still in love. She wanted more of those searing kisses, but instead she let her eyes wander through the open archways to the living room, the den, up the wide winding staircase toward the bedrooms upstairs. All the way to the balcony circling around the room. She turned all the way around, not wanting to miss a single detail.

"It's ready for you to put your touches on it, now, Violet," Orrin stepped back and folded his arms across his chest.

"What are you saying?" she asked.

"I'm saying I went away for eight years and made enough money to buy this land and build this house. The balcony is from one of the hotels I visited in San Francisco, California. I loved the way the bedrooms opened out and a body could look right down into the lobby. So I kind of fixed it like that. There's six bedrooms up there, Violet. Plenty for a house full of kids to slide down that stair railing and keep it polished. If there's too much here for you to keep cleaned up, I'll hire a whole staff of servants. All I ever wanted to do was farm, and that's what I'll do even though I don't have to. According to Alford, there's enough gold in the bank to keep me, my children, and my grandchildren until they all die."

"Are you saying?" She tried to fit all his words into a single sentence. Was he really telling her he'd built this mansion for her?

"I'm saying that I never quit loving you. I never thought I'd have another chance at life with you. Will you marry me?" He took her trembling hands in his and kissed her before she could answer. Just one more kiss, in case she told him to drop dead, that she'd never trust him again.

The world stood still for a moment as two lonely souls

found happiness. Violet shed the last thread of doubt, and Orrin found his answer in the kiss.

"Yes, Orrin, I will marry you," she said.

"When?" he whispered.

She smiled. "We'll talk about that later. Now will you please kiss me again. Just one more time beforc we go upstairs and see all those rooms we'll fill up with Wilde boys."

"How about Wilde girls?" he asked, his heart floating somewhere up above the clouds in the sky outside.

"Oh, there'll be plenty of them to keep Logan County in gossip and Anna Marie buying locks to keep her boys from coming to Dodsworth to do their courting." Violet laid her cheek on his chest and listened to the steady beat of his heart. She hoped she never lived a day past the time when that heart stopped beating. Without Orrin, life wasn't worth living.

"Anna Marie would do well to keep her little short boys away from my tall, beautiful daughters. Ain't a one of them would look cross-eyed at one of her boys anyway." He liked the way she fit so naturally into his arms. He hoped she didn't want one of those long engagements.

"I'm going to order a new stove and sewing machine." She leaned back and looked deeply into his eyes. "The money you paid me for this land is going to go into all the things I want for this house."

"I'll buy you whatever you want, and you don't have to work anymore at sewing either," he said.

"Orrin, I'm going to sew if I want to. I don't know how I'll ever have time with all this house to take care of plus a garden, but I'll sew if I want to. I'm not a withering flower that can't take the heat. I'm an independent woman and I don't intend to change," she vowed.

"Yes, ma'am," he said, grinning. "Now let's go look at the kitchen. And I'm having them build in a bathroom up-stairs, too, with one of those tubs that drain outside." He held her hand as they moved slowly through the living room toward the kitchen at the rear of the house.

"Orrin, it's huge!" Her gray eyes danced with excitement.

He slipped his arms around her waist and looked at the bare room from her eyes. "I thought you'd like room to work. Your little kitchen was so small you couldn't cuss a cat without getting fur in your mouth."

She threw back her head and laughed, a rich, resonant laugh that made him want to sing and dance. Life was good. Nothing could possibly go wrong now.

Chapter Fifteen

Happiness filled Violet's breast as she walked through the bedroom door and out onto the balcony. She had spent the night before in the cabin, but Emma insisted that Orrin stay at their house. Superstition had it that the bride and groom shouldn't see each other the day of the wedding, not until she walked down the aisle of the church. And Emma wasn't taking any chances on this wedding.

Violet thought she'd kept everything she needed when Orrin moved their belongings from the cabin to the new house. But when she began to get dressed, she didn't have the blue garter Emma had made for her, so she drove the buggy she planned to take to the church out to the house to retrieve her garter. She'd dressed too early out of nervousness. It had been four weeks since Orrin proposed that Sunday afternoon. They'd agreed they would marry when everything was in place and they could spend their honeymoon at their new home. The last thing had arrived just the day before. That was her new piano to grace the living room.

She ran her hand along the slick surface of the stair railing as she slowly descended to the main floor. A silver bowl filled with magnolia blossoms graced the foyer table. There would be a reception at the house right after the wedding ceremony at the church, and that's when she planned to give Orrin his wedding present. She'd ordered a brand new fiddle and planned that the two of them would make music for the guests like they had back in Blue Ridge. She took the fiddle from the case and laid it gently on her shoulder. She was tempted to run the bow down the strings just once, but she didn't. Orrin should play the fiddle first, just like she should make the piano ring with music.

A new royal blue settee with matching side chairs flanked the fireplace in the living room. Glass vases on the mantel held masses of every kind of flower Emma and the girls could find. Flower beds in and around Dodsworth had been robbed, as well as the countryside's offerings of wildflowers. Orrin picked out the dining room furniture. A long table with twelve matching chairs in a dark cherry wood polished to a high sheen. Two sideboards and a china cupboard completed the ensemble but didn't crowd the room. *We'd better have a dozen kids if we expect to ever fill up the whole house*, she thought as she made her way back to the kitchen.

The three-tiered wedding cake, along with several layer cakes so there would be enough to feed everyone who'd been invited to the wedding, waited on the kitchen table. Emma said Jed would carry them to the dining table at the last minute. She declared that child of Alford and Anna Marie's would knock it off the table the first thing when he arrived if they put it out before the time to cut it.

The big clock in the foyer chimed six times. The wedding was set for 7:00. Emma, Jed, and the kids were leaving for the church at 6:15 and she was supposed to drive herself at 6:30. That way, Orrin would be in the church ahead of her and wouldn't see her until she walked down the aisle.

She checked her reflection in the mirror. The simple ivory brocade two-piece dress showed off her ample bosom and her tiny waistline. She put her hands on her waist and wondered if Maggie had been a prophetess when she said that about the undergarments fitting until she got in the family way. Well, she didn't care if that happened on their wedding night. She was twenty-six years old and Orrin wanted a big family, so they'd better not waste any time.

She viewed the dress she and Emma had slaved over in the gold gilded mirror in the foyer. The bodice was accented with a peplum and a belt that tied in a bow at the small of her back. She'd almost left the bow off, since she was a twenty-six-year-old widow and not a blushing first-time bride. But Emma had declared it added something to the outfit. Three-quarter sleeves had a flounce ruffle with real storebought lace on the edge. The bustle skirt sported the slightest train. She'd twisted her hair up in a French roll up the back and laced a bit of baby's breath in the edges. Too many tongues would wag if she'd put a veil on her head.

She still wore John Whitebear's moccasins, but the dress had been hemmed long enough that they didn't show. Even though her feet were almost healed, she didn't think she could stand her lace-up shoes on for the whole evening. "Well, it's time. Eight years later than it should have been, but it's time," she told the smiling lady looking back at her in the mirror. She picked up her gloves and opened the front door to the most glorious evening of her life. Orrin was at the church this time, and she didn't doubt for one minute that their life would be wonderful. A few fights here and there to keep it spicy, and lots of kids to keep it busy. Someday they'd slow down and watch the second or third generation play on the lawn at the Wilde place. Maybe even the fourth of fifth if they lived long enough.

She wiped the dust from the buggy seat and hopped in, flicked the reins against her new horse's flanks, and turned him to head toward the church. Two miles and less than forty minutes and she'd be standing in front of the altar with Orrin. Then everyone would follow them home for wedding cake, homemade ice cream, and lots of dancing. Her fingers itched to play the piano, and her ears longed to hear the whine of a country boy's fiddle accompanying her.

Orrin's hands were clammy as he fiddled with the gold wedding band in the pocket of his brand new black three-pieced suit. He paced the ground behind the church and practiced his vows. "I take thee, Violet Daniels McDonald, to be my lawfully wedded wife, to have and to hold . . ."

"Nervous?" Jed asked, appearing from the front of the church. "It's only five more minutes and the show starts. The church is packed full. Looks like the whole county has turned out. Course we don't get weddings and invitations to receptions in a mansion very often around these parts. They're all as excited as if it were their own kids getting married."

"I'm so nervous I'm about to lose my supper," Orrin said, trying to smile. "This is what I've wanted for eight years, Jed. I knew I'd made a mistake in the first six weeks, but there wasn't any going back then. Violet's old daddy would have filled my Texas hide full of buckshot if I'd showed myself back in Blue Ridge. And I couldn't have blamed him. If someone did that to my daughter, I'd shoot him right between the eyes. Saint Peter wouldn't even put it down on my record."

"All's well that ends well." Jed patted him on the shoulder. "I forgot to tell you. Doc brought us a telegram when he came for the wedding. Emma's step-uncle is on the way. He says he's grateful for the land Violet donated and for the office you had built for him. He'll be here next week. Things have worked out just perfect with the cabin. I'm glad we didn't tear it down when we built the big house."

"Seems like it's blessed or something." Orrin smiled.

"First you and Emma settled your differences in that little place. Then me and Violet finally got things settled there. Think maybe the new doctor will find a true love in the same cabin."

"The doctor is already engaged to the daughter of one of the most prestigious men in the state of Georgia. I expect he'll be casting his eyes around to find a piece of property to build her a house pretty soon. Goodness knows from what Emma has said about Carolina Prescott, she wouldn't set foot in that little cabin," Jed said.

"Well, is it time? I'm ready to be a married man," Orrin said nervously.

"It's time. Me and you will walk in behind Preacher Elgin and go down the aisle to wait for Emma and then Violet. Looking back, I'm glad Emma and I got married at the sheriff's office," Jed said.

The two of them walked around the side of the church and met Preacher Elgin at the door. He nodded seriously and led the way into the church. Violet was to pull up the reins just down Main Street and wait until the church bells rang to drive on into the church yard. Just as Orrin reached the altar and turned to look into the smiling faces of all his newly found friends, Jimmy rang the bell. Three times. Loudly. Clearly. Five minutes and Violet would follow Emma into the church. Five minutes was only a few seconds short of sheer eternity to a man waiting at the front of the church with a case of nerves like Orrin had.

Violet heard the thunder of hooves coming toward her as she rounded the last curve into Dodsworth. John White-bear had changed his mind and was bringing his wife and their horde of kids to the wedding. She could have jumped out of the buggy and danced a jig. That would put the icing on the cake of a beautiful day.

It wasn't until the horses surrounded her buggy that she really looked up. Straight into the murderous black eyes of

Damian. He threw back his head and laughed as she grabbed the bridle of her horse and stopped the buggy. "So you are a hard woman to kill, giant woman. I heard in Guthrie that you survived my fire. Never thought you'd have the brains to figure out you could shoot the rope. Heard you ran through the flames. Maybe you were a cat in another lifetime and you have nine lives. Well, today you have used them all up."

"Get out of my way," she stared him right in the eye and demanded.

"Bring up the extra horse," Damian called out to Santos. "You wanted me to bring her to Mexico for your fun. Well, my friend, fate has given her to you. I do not like big women but you four can do whatever you like with this old lady. She's all dolled up and clean, so you can fight over who gets her the first day."

"I won't go anywhere with you," she whispered. Fear made her knees so weak she didn't think she could stand on them, but she hopped out of the buggy and started walking toward the church on the other end of town. Three loud bells rang. Orrin would be waiting at the front of the church. She lifted her skirts and started to run.

Damian's laugh rang out behind her just as a lasso floated down around her body. One tight jerk and her arms were pinned beside her body. It was over. She was so close to happiness and now she was the same as a dead woman. She turned quickly to spit in Damian's face, hoping that it infuriated him enough that he'd shoot her on the spot. Orrin's heart would break but it would be better than thinking that she'd run away and left him standing at the front of the church. He'd get over a death given time, but she remembered the ache of rejection and loved him too much to make him endure that kind of pain.

The last thing she saw was the butt of the pistol as Santos brought it down on her forehead. *Lord let me be dead*, she prayed as she hit the ground in a heap of ivory brocade.

She didn't feel the arms of the bandits as two of them tossed her over the extra horse and tied her to the saddle horn. If she'd heard the ribald comments they made, she would have willed herself to truly be dead.

"Let's ride. Now we really go to Mexico. We have the bank's gold and Orrin Wilde's woman. The devil has given us a good day." Damian dug his silver spurs into his horse and they all rode off, leaving nothing but an empty buggy and boiling dust in their wake.

Five minutes passed. Ten minutes. The congregation began to look back at the doors. Two more minutes and Orrin began to sweat in earnest. Surely Violet wouldn't leave him at the altar like he'd done her. She'd said she loved him. Night after night when he kissed her goodnight at the bedroom door. He'd heard her humming in the bedroom. She wouldn't have been happy if she'd been setting him for a fall like this.

"Orrin, was Violet running late?" Preacher Elgin asked in a whisper.

"No, she was supposed to be here. She knew just when to leave. We've driven it several times so she'd know just when to start," Orrin said, a blush creeping up his neck as he tapped one foot impatiently.

"Think we better go look for her?" Jed asked.

"She'll be here. Can we wait another five minutes? Maybe she didn't hear the bells," Orrin said. "Let's send Jimmy to ring them again. Could be she had trouble with the new horse and is waiting for the bells."

The back doors of the church flew open and Orrin sighed in relief. There was an explanation and they'd laugh about it later. He expected Emma in her new blue dress to fill the door, but instead the sheriff and a whole posse of men shoved their way into the church. Emma was amongst them, trying to run down the aisle to Jed, who had his arms outstretched.

"There's been a bank robbery in Guthrie. Five bandits

got away with everything. They're riding this way. Has anyone seen them? We were afraid they had you all held hostage when we found the buggy down the road." The sheriff's big voice boomed in the small church.

"It's Violet's buggy, Jed." Emma burst into tears. "They brought it in. There's a piece of her wedding dress material on the wheel. "They've taken her."

Orrin's pulse raced. His heart almost stopped beating. "How long ago? I'll go with you. Someone give me a gun."

Preacher Elgin reached under the pulpit and handed him a .22 rifle. "I left it here last week after I'd been squirrel hunting. Meant to take it home. Guess the Lord had other ideas."

"Who's the robbers?" Orrin asked as he followed the sheriff down the aisle.

"Some Mexican named Damian and his followers. Someone named Santos. Another named Gramps, and a white man named Matthew Cross. There's at least one more with them. I think he's Mexican, too. There's posters up for their arrest for one job they pulled in Louisiana last month and one in Texas a couple of weeks ago," the sheriff said.

"Matthew Cross." Emma heard the name and shuddered. Matthew Cross was the very man who she'd been running from when she left Georgia. It had taken her father a long time to realize the man was a villain with dollar signs in his eyes instead of love.

"Wait a minute, Sheriff," Jed said. "I'm going, too. My family is in as much danger as Orrin's if Matthew Cross is in the state." Jed remembered the day he came home from the fields to find Emma's father and Matthew demanding that she go back to Georgia with them. The cold mean look in Matthew's eyes still haunted him.

"We can use all the help we can get, son," the sheriff nodded at him.

"They're riding south. Trail is fresh around the buggy.

Carolyn Brown

Probably got about a fifteen minute lead on us," the sheriff said as they mounted up and rode hard out of town.

Orrin set his jaw firmly. He should have gone ahead and taken care of that vicious snake before now. One thing for sure, he'd better hope the sheriff found him before Orrin did or there wouldn't be anything left to bring back for a trial.

Chapter Sixteen

Violet was awake long before they pulled up the reins and stopped to rest. She kept her eyes shut tightly against the fading light of day and tried not to think about the pounding pain in her head. She'd be in far less danger if they thought she was still unconscious, so she didn't fight with Santos and Gramps as they manhandled her roughly from the horse. Santos had her around the shoulders and Gramps took her feet. They swung her off the horse like a bag of chicken feed and tossed her in a grassy area. No one else seemed concerned with Violet as they gathered round the horses. They all talked at once about just how far back the posse might be and how much money was actually in the saddlebags on one of the horses. As they moved to one side and began to argue, Violet barely opened one eye to see how far she was from them. They were gesturing wildly about what they should do next.

"Matthew, we have to divide it up and split the shares," Damian said loudly. "The posse is right on our tails. You should not have shot that clerk."

"You shot one in Louisiana, so don't tell me what to do," Matthew said. "We aren't splitting shares right now. Not until we stop for the night. Then you can take that ugly woman and go to Mexico. I've got enough now to keep me a while. I'm going back to Atlanta and rub old Jefferson Cummin's face in the fact I'm a rich man someday. He and his uppity daughter, Emma, will wish they hadn't been so quick to run me off when they realize just how wealthy I am." Matthew laughed cynically.

Good grief, Violet thought through the pain in her head. How did Matthew Cross get tangled up with those bandits? He was the very man who'd caused Emma to run away from home. Who'd been so mean to her when she and Jed were separated last year.

"Why don't you go back to Dodsworth and set up your own bank. Teach that other big woman who is boss. Might catch her out alone and teach her some real manners, like we're going to do with this one." Damian flipped his head toward Violet who lay very still as if she were dead. "I didn't think I would ever like a big woman, but she looks pretty nice in all that fine silk. I might take even take the first day and night for myself."

"I'd like to do that, but my face is posted on every wanted flier this side of the Mississippi," Matthew said, and chuckled again. "Five more minutes to rest these horses, and we're on the road again. I'm going to California. Until things blow over. I'd like to catch Emma out and make her pay for turning me into an outlaw, and maybe I will someday, but I won't be settin' up no bank in Oklahoma, I'm afraid."

"You won't try to ride away with all that gold, will you, amigo? I would hate to think I've got nothing to show for my work when I go home to Mexico. This time I have enough to keep me for the rest of my life, and I'm not leaving again. Who knows, maybe the big woman will choose to stay with me and keep me in my old age."

Gramps said. "We should each carry some of the money so one of us doesn't take off with it all."

"I'll carry it," Matthew said. "Trust me. I'm the brains behind this operation. You four wouldn't have the sense to pull off a robbery."

"That is enough." Damian jerked the bags from Matthew's horse and threw them down in the middle of the circle they'd made. Matthew bowed up to him, and the screaming match began in earnest. Four yelling in rapid Spanish and one in English. While their attention was diverted to the quality of honor amongst thieves, Violet rolled slowly toward a copse of trees just to her left. She opened one eye a slit to check on the situation and they were still at it, ignoring her and trying to settle their differences with volume. Damian jerked his hat from his heat and beat his leg with it, turning his back to her to argue some more. That's when she rose to her feet and ran the last ten feet into the wooded area. Her head ached and green briers tore at her wedding dress but she kept moving deeper and deeper into the trees.

"Where is the woman?" she heard Santos yell excitedly at the same time she felt the thunder of many hooves through the soft deerskin of her moccasins. It sounded like some came from the north and another set rode from the south. The bandits jumped on their horses and split seven ways to Sunday, leaving the bags on the ground in their haste. She turned in time to see Damian give one last glance toward the trees as he tried to outrun five or six horses surrounding him. John Whitebear reached out and deftly knocked Damian from his horse, and was on top of him with a rope tying his hands behind his back before Damian could catch the breath he lost when he hit the ground. Four braves tied his feet to his hands and left him with another one as guard while they rode off in pursuit of Matthew Cross, who'd ridden as far as he could go without convincing his horse to climb a tree.

Violet began to shake all over as she watched the whole foray from her hiding spot. By the time the sheriff brought his posse to a stop where the saddlebags were laying with the bank money, the Indians had Matthew Cross trussed up like a Thanksgiving turkey. One shot had been fired, and Matthew had fired that one—just before John threw out his arm and knocked Matthew hind end over tea kettle into a patch of poison ivy and green briers.

"Here's your money." One of the posse handed the bags to the sheriff. "Looks like the Indians got two of them. We'll ride south and catch the other three."

"Where's Violet?" Orrin dismounted in a dead run toward Damian. He kicked Damian over onto his side and put the barrel of the gun in his chest. "Where's Violet?" he demanded.

The Mexican smiled, showing off stained teeth. "Your giant woman went with the rest of them. When they figure out they have lost the money again, she will have to pay dearly."

Orrin's trigger finger twitched. "Don't do it, son," the sheriff said. "He's trying to rile you. Give me the gun. We'll take him back to jail. He's going to hang. He killed a man in the Louisiana robbery. Witnesses say he shot him out of spite on the way out of the bank. Don't take the law into your hands, Orrin."

Beads of sweat pooled up on Orrin's forehead. He took his finger from the trigger but he didn't give the sheriff the gun. "I'm riding south with the rest of them. I've got to find her."

"Orrin," he heard the plaintive cry from the woods and jerked his head around, his eyes searching the tree line. It had to be his imagination. The Mexican said the other three took her with them. Unless it was a trap. One of them might have her at gun point and when he approached they'd shoot him full of holes.

Violet could no more make her legs carry her out of the

woods than she could have sprouted wings and flown to his side right then. The rope still held her arms tight against her body and she was shivering from head to toe in spite of the summer heat. "Orrin," she called out again and watched as he threw the gun down and began to run. He'd use his bare hands to beat the man holding his Violet to a bloody pulp. The fool would wish he was dead by the time Orrin vented his pent-up rage on him. The sheriff just shook his head. If one of the bandits was holding Violet McDonald hostage then he felt sorry for the man. He just hoped he didn't shoot Orrin Wilde. The man had brought a lot to Oklahoma with him. Why, the sheriff wouldn't be a bit surprised to see Orrin's name on the first set of senators when Oklahoma became the state it was destined to be.

"Are you alone, Violet?" the sheriff called out.

"Yes, sir," her voice carried to his ears.

"No one is in there with you?"

"No one," Violet said, her head aching and the trees fast becoming a blur.

Orrin gathered her into his arms and held her trembling body close to his. When he'd assured himself that she was alive, he cut the rope from her and held her tightly to his chest again. He'd never let her out of his sight again.

"My dress is ruined," she said.

"We'll buy another one. You are alive. Did they . . . ?"

"No, Orrin. They hit me with a pistol. They tied me up, threw me over a horse, and hit me on the head. That's what the bruise is. But they didn't harm me other than that. Please take me home," she begged, drawing strength from his arms and the beating of his heart.

"Orrin, did you find her?" Jed called out from the edge of the woods.

"Yes, she's here," Orrin yelled back.

"We got the other three as they fled south," Jed called out, walking toward the voices as he did. "Is Violet safe?"

"I'm fine, Jed. One of those men was that horrible Matthew Cross that hurt Emma," she said when Jed reached their sides.

"Hurt Emma?" Jed's eyes narrowed.

"Yes . . . uh oh," Violet stammered. She wasn't supposed to tell that story. Emma had sworn her to secrecy, fearing that Jed would feel honor bound to hunt the man down for slapping Emma and for the things he'd said to her. "Emma will have to tell you about it, Jed. I can't. I've said too much."

"Where is the varmint?" Jed drew a pistol from his belt.

"He's over there with one of John Whitebear's braves." Orrin pointed. "But you're not going to shoot him. He's not worth losing your family over, man. Put the gun away and let the law take care of it."

"When?" Jed looked Violet in the eye and demanded answers.

"He slapped her when she was in Georgia. Her father caused him to loose his job at the bank because of it, and the rest is just ugly things he said to her. Nothing more, Jed, honest." Violet began to shake again.

"You're telling me the truth?" Jed searched her eyes.

"I swear." Violet reached out and touched his arm. "Can we just go home now?"

"I think we better. The wedding guests are all gone, Violet. I guess we'll have to reschedule the wedding," Jed said seriously. So Matthew Cross had met his end, just like Damian. And right here in Oklahoma Indian Territory. What goes around surely did come back around.

"I don't hardly think I could get married today anyway." Violet couldn't control the shaking. Everything started spinning in circles and she heard a faraway voice scream her name as her knees buckled and she slid out of Orrin's arms to the ground.

* * *

A soft summer breeze blew through the windows in her bedroom at the cabin when she opened her eyes again. Had it all been a horrible dream? She touched her head and the knot there told her it had been very real. Someone held her hand tightly and she rolled her head to the side to find Orrin sleeping beside her. Fully clothed still in his wedding shirt and trousers. Someone had removed her ragged wedding dress and redressed her in a nightgown of soft batiste. Probably Emma, she thought. A cool cotton sheet covered her all the way to her armpits. Strange, she'd slept with Orrin several times now, but she'd always been under the covers, and he'd been on top of them. It was time they shared a bed and a life.

But would it ever happen?

Once Orrin had walked out on her. The next time they tried to marry she'd been abducted and carried away. Maybe God was trying to tell her that she didn't need to marry Orrin after all. She looked at his handsome features in the moonlight and decided that it wasn't God meddling in her affairs at all. He might be testing their love, and if that was the case then they'd both just passed the tests with flying colors. But they were meant to be together, and by golly they would be. As soon as she recovered from the bump on her head, they would get married. They might just simply take a trip to the sheriff's office like Emma and Jed had done. Or call the preacher to bring the license to the house tomorrow morning and marry them right there in the cabin.

The third time is the charm, she thought just before she closed her eyes. *And it won't be at a church either. Not with a fancy dress or an altar to wait before. Next time it'll be my way, and it will work*, she promised herself as a deep peaceful sleep finally overtook her. As she fell asleep she tightened her hold on Orrin's hand. She'd never let him go . . . not ever.

Chapter Seventeen

Violet put the finishing touches on a three-layered chocolate cake in the kitchen. One strand of dark hair kept
sneaking away from the bun at the nape of her neck. Orrin
reached across the table and tucked it back for her. Just the
brush of his hand across her face and neck made her shiver.
She hoped she would always respond to his touch like that.
When she was ninety and wearing spectacles to see how to
sew, she wanted him to push back a strand of gray hair and
make her shiver.

The clock chimed seven times, and she leaned across the
table and kissed him soundly on the lips. "Guess I'd better
take my apron off now," she said, tugging the knot at the
small of her back. She tossed the apron over the back of a
kitchen chair and smoothed the front of her blue and white
gingham checked day dress. The only difference in it and
what she wore everyday was the puffy sleeves and the bustle she'd decided to wear at the last moment. There wasn't
even a touch of lace on the collar or around the edge of
the three-quarter sleeves.

"You're beautiful." Orrin guided her toward the door with his arm around her waist. "Even more so than you were last week in your other wedding dress."

"Well, thank you, Orrin. I've had two fancy dresses and neither of them worked. I didn't want to take a chance," she said.

"It isn't the dress that makes the woman, Violet. It's the woman that makes the dress. You could wear a gunny sack and still be beautiful," he told her honestly.

Emma and Jed motioned to them from the doorway into the dining room. "It's time," Jed said. "The tables are full of food, and folks are waiting."

"Ready?" Orrin asked.

"Been ready since you proposed that Sunday." Violet took his hand, and the two of them joined Jed and Emma and Preacher Elgin in the living room.

"The quickest ceremony you've got," Jed reminded Preacher Elgin. "We don't want anything to happen this time."

"I understand." Preacher Elgin nodded. "Dearly beloved, we are gathered today in the presence of God and these two close friends to join Violet McDonald and Orrin Wilde in holy matrimony."

They exchanged vows as well as plain gold wedding bands, and in five minutes Preacher Elgin finished the ceremony with, "By the authority vested in me in Oklahoma Indian Territory and the Almighty God, I pronounce you man and wife. Orrin, you may now claim your bride with a kiss."

Orrin looked to the depths of those mesmerizing gray eyes, into Violet's soul, and found a love there he'd never imagined could be his again. "I love you, Mrs. Wilde," he whispered as his lips met hers in a kiss that sealed their love forever.

"I love you, Orrin," she whispered back when his mouth reluctantly left hers.

"Congratulations," Jed and Emma chorused at the same time. "Now let's go outside and join the rest of the community for the reception."

Preacher Elgin preceded them to the front porch and rang a bell to get everyone's attention. "I would like to be the first to present Mr. and Mrs. Orrin Wilde to you," he said, grinning.

Orrin and Violet walked out the doors of their new white home to the thunder of applause. "Thank you," Orrin said. "We are glad you could all join us today for this important day. The tables are laid and if anyone goes home hungry they might not be able to get into Heaven, because that would be a sin. We'll start the music for the dancing at eight o'clock. Violet and I will lead with the first dance, and then I've got Violet talked into playing some mean Texas-style piano for you to dance to."

"A senator for sure," the sheriff said, shaking hands with both of them. "You ever think about politics, son?"

"Nope, I'm going to farm this land. Run a few coon dogs and maybe train up Missy to be a good bird dog," he said, shaking his head and leading Violet down the steps to join their friends in the yard.

"I was so worried something else would happen," Maggie said, hugging Violet. "Did you see that new doctor yet?"

"Yes, he arrived yesterday. Stayed at Emma's until we could get our things out of the cabin today. Got here earlier than we figured," Violet said.

"Oh, well, he's engaged, and I heard he can't dance no better than Ivan." Maggie giggled and took her place behind the cake table where Emma put the three-tiered chocolate cake in the middle of all the other cakes. "I guess it's time for you two to cut the first cake so we can all begin to eat."

"Yes, it is," Emma said. "Come on over here and cut a

piece out and then feed it to Orrin. Be careful though, if you get any on his face, it's sure to bring bad luck."

Violet laid her hand over Orrin's, and the two of them cut a wedge of chocolate cake. Orrin dragged a chair to a shade tree and sat down in it, playing his part of the pampered husband to the amusement of all the guests. Violet backed up and sat down in his lap and commenced to feed him with her fingers, breaking off a piece of cake and carefully putting it in his mouth.

"What happens if I get it all over my hands, Emma?" she asked.

"You won't." Orrin picked up her fingers and licked the icing off.

Goosebumps the size of gumballs rose up on her scalp and tickled their way down her arms. "Oops," she deliberately dropped a piece of icing which he caught in the palm of his hand before it hit the ground. "I guess turn about is fair play," she murmured as she picked up his hand and licked away the icing.

Orrin sucked air for several seconds and whispered under his breath, "You did that on purpose."

"Never underestimate me, Orrin," she said between her teeth and a brilliant smile.

"I'll remember that," he said, picking up a piece of cake and feeding her. "This is a two way street, folks," he announced. "I intend to spoil her as much as I expect to be spoiled."

When they finished the cake, Violet and Orrin were ushered to the tables to be the first in line for supper. Jed had barbecued half an Angus steer. John Whitebear brought a spit-roasted hog. Still in the husks, corn on the cob heated up in a pit of live coals. John's son, Thomas, shucked the corn and handed it to his mother, who buttered it with sweet cream butter she'd made the day before. The ladies of the area contributed bowls of potato salad, beans, cole slaw, sweet carrots, and so many desserts it was staggering. The whole affair was even better than the church socials where everyone brought their own lunch and ate on their quilts.

Jed and Emma were the first ones to stop by the table Emma had set up special for Violet and Orrin. "We are glad you are our neighbors and friends," Emma said. "I guess I can quit worrying now that something else would go wrong to keep this marriage from happening."

"Yes, you can," Orrin said. "Well, there's Anna Marie and Alford. A little late, but they made it," he said, noticing their wagon turning into the yard. "You know what, I think I'll let little Alford have first chance at Lalie Joy and save my daughters for someone else."

"Hey, I thought you were my friend," Jed slapped at him. "That little short, ornery boy better keep his distance from our part of Logan County if he wants to live to see old age."

"Oh, hush," Emma said. "Lalie Joy will have better sense than that. You did, even if it did take a lot of persuasion."

Orrin and Violet both laughed as their friends moved on to allow others their turn at the table. "Mrs. Wilde, I want to offer my congratulations," Ivan stopped and said next.

"Thank you, Ivan." Violet smiled up at him. "Maybe we'll be having a wedding feast for you before long."

Ivan shook his head. "I don't think so. I haven't found someone who will make a good wife yet. Mr. Wilde has got the best woman in all of Logan County."

"That I have, and thank you for the compliment." Orrin chuckled.

"Violet and Orrin, congratulations." Elenor Listen stopped by the table after Ivan had left. "I wish Maggie would hurry up and find someone to hitch up with so I could have a wedding. Momma says the oldest daughter has to marry first, and I've got my eye on Ivan."

"Oh?" Violet raised an eyebrow.

"Don't tell him," Elenor whispered. "He's already running so fast I might not catch him."

"We'd like to offer our congratulations," Alford said as he led Anna Marie to the table. "We're glad you decided to stay in Logan County."

"You have a lovely home," Anna Marie said, eyeing the mansion behind the bride and groom. "You've done good for a widow woman with no hope, Violet. Make the best of it." She walked away with her nose in the air.

"I'm sorry," Alford apologized.

"That's just Anna Marie." Violet smiled.

"Don't I know it." Alford rolled his eyes.

"So you've done good?" Orrin raised an eyebrow at his new wife.

"Yep, I just married you for your money. If you don't believe me, ask Anna Marie. Of course, I kind of like the way you turn my insides to jelly when you kiss me, too," she said.

Orrin grinned. His prayers had surely been answered.

When they'd finished eating, Orrin announced that he and Violet were ready to open the dancing with the first dance of the evening. Emma had graciously offered to play for them. It was a slow waltz, and even Maggie was awed by the sight of Orrin and Violet together under the first blinking stars as they moved together in unison.

"It's perfect," Violet said as she laid her head on Orrin's chest.

"We should have realized long ago that we are not the conventional couple," he whispered into her hair. Later he would take every one of those pins out one by one and enjoy watching all that dark hair float down over her shoulders.

"What does that mean?"

"Don't see the bride before the wedding. Get married in a church. All those things. We tried it that way, but our way seems to be working much better," he said.

"Let's always do it our way," she said as the dance ended

and she raised her lips to his for a very public, yet very passionate kiss.

"And now I will play for the dance," she announced when she took over Emma's place at the piano. "But before I begin, I would like to give my new husband a gift. I wouldn't think of letting him dance with all the women here tonight when I've just barely gotten him roped and branded. So, Orrin Wilde, if you'll join me?" She held out her hand.

"What's this all about?" he asked.

"When we were kids we used to play for lots of country dances. Me on the piano, Orrin with his fiddle. So I bought him a brand new fiddle. He can make a fiddle do everything but stand up and tell you bedtime stories. Now between the two of us, we'll get this dance started," she said.

Orrin took the fiddle from her hands. The stars in the sky couldn't compare with the twinkle in his eyes as he drew the bow across the strings and began a fast tune which Violet picked up on the piano. He leaned down and kissed her without missing a single note and said, "I really do love you, Violet. Thank you for the present."

They made beautiful music together for hours before the party finally wound down and the last guest loaded their dishes and kids into the wagons and went home. Maggie danced the last dance of the evening with the new doctor. Just before she crawled into the back of her father's wagon with her two sisters, she hugged Violet one more time. "I'm glad he's engaged. He stepped on my toes twice while we was dancing. And he don't talk about nothing but his doctoring. In his own way, he's just as dull as old Jim Parsons," she whispered conspiratorially and ran across the lawn to join her two sisters in the back of Mr. Listen's wagon.

Orrin picked Violet up and carried her over the threshold and up the stairs to their bedroom. He sat her on the edge of the bed, kneeled in front of her, and took both her hands in his. "I love you, Violet. I promise to love and cherish you all the rest of our lives, and those are not ever going to be forsaken vows."

"I love you, Orrin. I'm glad we've got another chance to be together. I promise to cherish and love you through this life and the one to come," she said.

He leaned forward and she met him half way. The kiss they shared lit up the room in a glittering glow. When it ended and he wrapped his arms around her for a hug, she remembered the words she'd prayed that night when Orrin fell on her porch.

"Lord, please. Can't I have someone more fervent than Jim Parsons in my life? Someone with a twinkle in his eyes and a passion in his heart. Someone who'll put a glitter in my eyes and who'll wake my restless heart to . . ."

She looked out the window beyond the stars and moon and mouthed the words, "Thank you."